Children's Stories

from

The Village Shepherd

Vol. II

Janice B Scott

Children's Stories

from  The Village Shepherd

Vol. II

Janice B. Scott

CSS Publishing Company
Lima, Ohio

CHILDREN'S STORIES FROM THE VILLAGE SHEPHERD, VOLUME II

FIRST EDITION
Copyright © 2012
by CSS Publishing Co., Inc.

For more information about CSS Publishing Company resources, visit our website at www. csspub.com, email us at csr@csspub.com, or call (800) 241-4056.

ISBN-13: 978-0-7880-2682-9
ISBN-10: 0-7880-2682-8

PRINTED IN USA

To Claire

Contents

Foreword

This second volume of short stories from The Village Shepherd is based on year C (the third year of the three-year cycle) of the Revised Common Lectionary, that is, the Bible readings selected for Sundays and used worldwide by mainstream Christian churches.

Each story is based on the gospel reading set for the Sunday. All the stories are suitable for use in church, although this collection is titled "Children's Stories," the stories can be enjoyed at a different level by adults.

Some familiar characters from Volume 1, like Praxis, the naughty pixie whose skin changes colour according to his moods, have marched into Volume 2 demanding to be heard. Other characters, like Roly the cuddly puppy, tentatively poke their heads around the door for the first time in this volume. Like the first volume, some of the stories are humorous, some have sadness within them, and some are full of joy. There are stories about success and failure, about bullying and hurt, about love and anger, joy and despondency, but above all, every story relates in some way to God and God's deep, unconditional love for each one of us.

That said the stories are not very religious but are earthed in real life, even though that life — like that of fairies and pixies, gnomes and goblins — may be imaginary. The theme is usually obvious but the way the story relates to the Bible passage may be less obvious and occasionally may require some digging on the part of the reader.

A few of the stories are not original but are retellings of ancient legends because these stories contain deep truths that have already been beautifully expressed. "The Parable of Bamboo" is one such legend, providing a wonderful means of understanding the Easter story, and the two Christmas stories, "The Spider's Web" and "The Christmas Thorn of Glastonbury" are well known and well loved tales. "Oscar's Courage" is a simplified version of the story of Oscar Romero, the Archbishop of El Salvador who was martyred for his stand on behalf of the poor.

Most of these stories are suitable for primary age children upward, but one or two — such as "Oscar's Courage" and "The Big City" — are perhaps more suitable for older children or teenagers.

As we move further away in time from the first century, so the gap between those who choose to attend church and those who do not is widening until it is not far short of an abyss. I believe we need to urgently find ways to bridge this abyss, so the aim of this little volume is to present the good news of Jesus Christ in a way that can be heard and understood by this present generation. It has been my experience that a life including God is a life full of fun, love, and enjoyment, even though things may not always go entirely smoothly. Even in the bad times when I cling onto faith by my fingertips, I am aware that God's strong arms are holding me and that the fun and happiness are not so far away. It is my profound hope that all readers of this volume may experience that for themselves.

Roly Interprets the Signs

Luke 21:25-36

This is a difficult reading for adults, never mind children! So to-day's story is a simple story about Roly, an abandoned puppy who interprets various signs as meaning he is about to enjoy a very special day indeed.

Roly lay on the stone floor with his head on his paws. He wondered how much longer it was until it was time for food. Feeding time was the best time in the whole day, because then the humans came and rubbed his head and spoke to him and made a fuss of him.

Roly had lived in the Dogs' Home all his short life. He had a vague memory of a warm mother dog, against whom he used to snuggle with some other tiny puppies. But his next memory was of being pulled out of a river in a dripping, wet sack. Then he had arrived at the Dogs' Home where he had lived ever since.

The Dogs' Home people had called him Roly because of his long, round body and his tiny legs. He quite liked it in the Dogs' Home, because there were lots of other dogs of all different shapes and sizes, and it was good to be in company. And the humans were kind to him. But there were so many dogs to look after, that Roly often felt lonely and bored.

But today was different. Today Roly had woken with a feeling of anticipation, as though something special was going to happen. The humans who fed him in the early morning had seemed a bit happier than usual, although Roly had no idea why.

"Today's the day for one of you," one of the humans had remarked. "I wonder whose lucky day it is today?" And although he didn't know what that meant, Roly hoped and hoped it would be his lucky day.

Soon there was a great commotion in the Dogs' Home. All the different dogs were getting very excited, and Roly soon found himself jumping up and down as high as his little legs would carry him and yapping and barking at the top of his voice. He wasn't sure why he was acting in this way, but he certainly was aware of great excitement in the air.

After a while, the door to the kennels opened and some strange humans came in. Some were normal sized humans, but three of them were very small humans with high voices. Roly liked the look of the little humans, and he began to bark more urgently and started to chase his tail just to capture their attention.

The little girl came and knelt at his cage. "Oh look!" she cried to her brothers. "This is a dear little dachshund. Do let's have him!"

Roly wasn't sure what she meant, but he was sure that she was a kind child, and he knew that he wanted desperately to stay with her. He sat in front of her with his head on one side and gazed beseechingly into her eyes. Then he gently began to lick her hand through the wires of the cage.

The two boys came over to join their sister, but Roly instinctively felt they would be more interested in a robust display of gymnastics. So he began to jump and turn and race around his cage.

"I really wanted a bigger dog," one of the boys said.

Roly immediately felt very anxious. He was the smallest dog in the Dogs' Home, and he knew he couldn't compete with Labradors and Retrievers, Boxers and Bulldogs.

The girl turned to her parents. "*Please*," she said putting her hand into her father's and gazing into his eyes just as Roly had gazed into hers.

Roly wondered whether he had interpreted the signs right. Was this a special day for him? Or had he got it wrong? Perhaps it was a special day for some other dog. He lay down again and put his head on his paws, but he kept one eye on the little family.

The girl's mother said, "He does look awfully well behaved. And they say all the dogs are house-trained. Let's take him!"

And Roly knew that the signs were right and he was about to begin a new life.

Roly Makes a Straight Path

Luke 3:1-6

> *This is a story designed to relate the "making of a straight path" to everyday life. Lots of situations are bewildering and frightening for children, but salvation comes in unexpected ways. In this story, Roly the puppy "makes the path straight" for Alice because he can instinctively follow a scent.*

Roly lay down with his head on his paws and felt lonely. But he wasn't lonely for long, for lots of people came to the entrance to the maze and petted him and patted him and stroked him and spoke to him. Roly perked up and wondered for the hundredth time what went on in a maze. Still, the family had told him very firmly to stay at the entrance in case he got lost in the maze, or worse, because he was so small, tripped people up by darting between their legs.

But suddenly, Roly pricked up his ears. He had heard a faint sob, and he knew immediately it was Alice. Before he had time to think he was off, racing into the maze, squeezing through small gaps at the bottom of the maze hedges and following Alice's scent. He found her very quickly and snuggled up to her, licking her hand to tell her how much he loved her.

Her brothers had run off laughing, leaving Alice somewhere in the maze all by herself. Alice had no idea which way to turn. At first she had tried to find her way to the centre of the maze, but she kept coming back to the same place and could neither find her way to the centre nor out again. Hence the tears, for it's very frightening when all you can see are tall hedges on either side and you can't find your way when you're all alone.

But it wasn't frightening for Roly. Dachshunds used to be hunting dogs, and although Roly had never hunted in his entire life, he had been born with the right instincts. He set off at a dash, wriggling under hedges and scraping through tiny spaces, with Alice close behind. As the smallest and youngest of the three children, Alice was still small enough to wriggle through any holes in the maze hedges.

They didn't follow the conventional route of the pathways to the centre of the maze, but they reached the centre by a much more direct route and were waiting when the boys eventually managed to find their way there.

The boys were stunned. They had expected to pick up their little sister on the return journey, for they had been quite sure she would never find her way by herself. Unnoticed, Roly slipped quietly back to the entrance. And Alice never did tell her brothers how she had found her way to the centre of the maze.

Roly Shows the Way

Luke 3:7-18

*At times we all behave badly and often don't realise until later
what harm our behaviour has done. John the Baptist exhorted
people to follow the true way, the way of Jesus. In this story, Roly the
puppy shows the three children the right way to behave.*

The three children were racing through the woods, and Roly was keeping up as best he could with his short legs. He was a reluctant participant in this escapade, for even though he loved nothing better than the woods, he had an inkling of what the children were about.

There was a battered old caravan standing in a glade deep in the woods. The children had come across it one day and had amused themselves peering in the gloomy windows and scrawling rude words on the dirty paintwork.

When the owner of the caravan, a derelict old man complete with long, unkempt beard, had suddenly materialised from the woods shouting and brandishing his fist at them, the children had run away laughing.

Since then, they had discovered the old man to be a constant source of amusement. So at every opportunity they raced to the woods to plague the old man. All three of them had high voices that carried well and irritated the old man beyond endurance. But the children were quick and nimble on their feet, so there was never any danger of the old man catching them.

It was only Roly the puppy who seemed to feel uneasy about the children's pranks. Having experienced ill treatment himself in his youngest days, Roly disliked being part of anything that might hurt or upset another creature, even when it was just fun. So today his heart was a little heavy even as he flew after the children as fast as he could.

But today the children were doomed to disappointment. The caravan appeared to be deserted for the old man was nowhere to be seen. No matter how much the children danced around singing silly songs and shouting rude remarks, nothing happened.

"Come on," said Jem, the oldest. "We might as well go home. There's no fun here today, the daft old fool's not around."

The other two turned to follow him, but Roly's sharp ears picked up a faint murmur unheard by the children. He began to bark, urgently.

"Oh do come on, Roly," called Jem. "We don't want to wait around here for you."

But Roly ran up to the door of the caravan and began to scratch at it with his sharp little claws. He whined and barked and yapped, anxious for the children to come and see what he was about.

Alice turned back. "I think he wants us to go to the caravan," she said.

"Don't be stupid, Alice," growled Jem. "He's only a silly puppy. What does he know?"

But Alice had already run over to Roly at the caravan. As Roly anxiously pawed at the door, she grasped the handle and turned it. The children had never been inside the caravan before, so it was a shock to Alice to see the state of the van. It was dingy inside, but as Alice's eyes grew accustomed to the dim light she could see that the van was piled high with old newspapers, dirty washing, and unwashed crocks.

She called her brothers over, and together they entered the van. Then they all heard a faint groan. Underneath a pile of rags on the bed, was the old man. He was only semi-conscious.

"What shall we do?" asked Alice, suddenly frightened.

Jem took charge. "One of us must stay here and do the best we can for him, poor old fellow. The other two must run for help."

Alice was terrified, for the old man looked as though he might die at any moment. But she knew both her brothers were much faster runners than she was, so she would have to stay while they went for help. Almost asked if he knew what she was thinking, Roly jumped up and licked her hand.

Alice immediately felt better. While they were waiting for the boys to return with adult help, Roly jumped onto the old man's bed, and began to lick his face. After a while, the old man's eyes flickered and opened. When he spotted Alice he groaned and closed his eyes again. Alice felt deeply ashamed of her previous behaviour. But she quickly poured some water into a bowl, found an old cloth, and began to wash the old man's face.

His eyes flickered open again, and this time he looked astonished.

"I'm sorry we were so nasty to you," muttered Alice, her lip trembling. "We didn't know you were ill. My brothers have gone to fetch help. You'll soon be all right."

The old man was taken to hospital, where he made a complete recovery. While he was in hospital the three children set about cleaning up his caravan and restoring order inside it. They were all very ashamed of the way they had behaved and wanted to make amends.

"Roly showed us the way," remarked Alice. "I don't think Roly was ever very happy about the way we teased the old man. And if it hadn't been for Roly, the old man would have died."

After the old man came out of hospital the children got to know him really well. They discovered that they liked him a lot, and even more surprising, he liked them. When they tentatively told him how sorry they were for teasing him so mercilessly, he just smiled and said, "I was young once myself. And I reckon you saved my life, thanks to that puppy of yours, so now we're quits. But you keep on the straight path, you kids. Believe me, that's the only path to be on. Follow that all your lives, and you won't go far wrong."

And the children did just what he said.

Roly's First Christmas

Luke 1:39-45

> *This is the final story in the group of four Advent stories about Roly the puppy. In this story, Roly discovers the meaning of Christmas for himself.*

Roly the dachshund puppy was feeling rather bewildered. He had just been getting used to his new family when something called "Christmas" seemed to be arriving. It was very upsetting, for the children were over-excited which meant there were lots of quarrels and bickering.

Roly didn't know why they were so excited, but he had a feeling something special was about to happen. The last time he'd had this feeling was when the family had found him in the Dogs' Home and had brought him here, to this new home. Roly hoped the feeling didn't mean he was going to have to move on again. But he felt a little uneasy and rather frightened, so he hid under the table whenever he heard raised voices.

One day, the family brought a tree into the house. Roly couldn't believe his eyes. Everyone, even small puppies, knew that trees belonged outside! Why on earth should the family bring a tree indoors? It was even stranger when the family began to decorate the tree. The boys, who were taller than Alice, put a little angel on the top of the tree, and draped the tree with brightly coloured lights. Alice hung glass baubles and tiny ornaments on all the branches she could reach. Then the children adorned the tree with tinsel from top to bottom.

Even Roly could see how grand the tree looked. Later, brightly wrapped packages and parcels of all shapes and sizes appeared at the foot of the tree. Roly sniffed and snuffled and explored with his nose, but was immediately shouted at by the family. He wasn't sure what he'd done wrong, but he realised the packages weren't for him so he retired under the table again.

Roly wasn't sure he liked Christmas very much. He wished everything would return to normal, when he could play with the children and trees lived outside the house where they belonged.

But when Christmas Day dawned, Roly discovered his food bowl was filled with all sorts of enticing things to eat. He began to think perhaps Christmas wasn't so bad after all. And when at lunchtime his bowl was refilled with something called "turkey," he gradually began to enjoy himself.

After lunch the family began to open all the parcels underneath the Christmas tree. Roly was afraid he might be shouted at again, so he hid beneath the table. But then he heard Alice calling him, so he ventured out onto the rug in front of the fire. Alice placed one of the parcels in front of him.

Roly looked up at her enquiringly, unsure what he was supposed to do.

"Come on, Roly," said Alice encouragingly. "This one is yours. It's my Christmas present to you, so you can open this one."

Roly put his head on one side. He wasn't entirely sure what she had said, but her voice sounded really kind so he began to tentatively snuffle at the parcel. When this didn't produce any shouts, he began to tear at the coloured paper with his teeth. Inside the parcel were some Doggy chews, some Doggy chocolate drops, a rubber toy that squeaked when he held it with his teeth, and a huge rubber bone. Roly was so excited that he began to play all over the room with his rubber toy, while the family laughed and cheered him on.

When he was tired out, Roly lay down on the rug in front of the fire and Alice came and lay beside him. Roly snuggled up to Alice, who put her arm around him. Roly felt completely, ecstatically happy. He couldn't remember ever having been so happy before. And suddenly he realised what Christmas was all about.

It was all about love, the love he felt in this family even if they occasionally shouted at him. And especially the love he felt from Alice and the love he felt for Alice. And as he fell asleep at the end of his first Christmas Day, Roly knew that for a puppy like him, the most important thing in the whole world was love.

The Christmas Thorn
of Glastonbury

Luke 2:1-20

After baby Jesus grew up to be a man, he got into terrible trouble and wicked people killed him. But a good man called Joseph of Arimathea laid Jesus' body gently in his own grave, which he'd made ready for when he should die. After that the wicked people searched for Joseph of Arimathea, and so he ran away from Jerusalem carrying with him a special cup, which contained some of Jesus' holy blood.

The cup was called the Holy Grail and Joseph carried it hidden beneath a mystical, white cloth. For many moons he wandered, leaning on his staff cut from a white-thorn bush. He passed over raging seas and dreary deserts, he wandered through forests, climbed rugged mountains, and waded through many floods.

At last he came to France where the Apostle Philip was telling the people about Jesus. So Joseph stayed there for a little while. One night while Joseph lay asleep in his hut, he was wakened by a radiant light. He rubbed his eyes and sat up, and there was an angel standing by his bed. "Joseph of Arimathea," said the angel, "cross over into England and preach the glad tidings about Jesus to the people there. And there, when you see a special Christmas miracle, build the first Christian church in England." Joseph lay there puzzled and a bit frightened and wondering what he should do, for in those days it was a very dangerous sea voyage from France to England, and England itself was said to be a dangerous place.

So he left his hut and calling his friend the Apostle Philip, told Philip the angel's message. When morning came, Philip sent Joseph on his way, with eleven chosen men to help him. They went down to the water's side, and embarking in a little ship, they set out on the sea. After a long, long voyage, at last they came to the coast of England.

They were met there by people who knew nothing about Jesus. So Joseph of Arimathea told them all about Jesus, the tiny baby born in the manger, and about Jesus' life when he grew up, and about his death on a cross. The King of England liked what he heard, so he gave Joseph and his followers a place called Avalon, which means "the happy isle," and he told them to go there straightaway and to build there an altar to God.

Avalon was a wonderful place. It was beautiful and peaceful. It lay deep in the middle of a green valley. Trees of delicious fruit and gorgeous, scented flowers grew in the valley. Smooth waves gently lapped the shore, and water-lilies floated on the surface of the tide; while in the blue sky above sailed fleecy clouds.

Joseph and his companions reached the Isle of Avalon on Christmas Eve. With them they carried the Holy Grail hidden beneath its snow-white cloth. Heavily they toiled up the steep hill. When they reached the top, Joseph thrust his thorn-staff into the ground and immediately a miracle happened. The thorn-staff instantly put down roots, sprouted and budded, and burst into a mass of white and fragrant flowers!

On that very spot where the thorn had bloomed, just as he'd been told by the angel, Joseph built the first Christian church in England. In the church they placed the Holy Grail, and ever since then, at Glastonbury Abbey — the name by which Avalon is known today — on Christmas Eve the white thorn buds and blooms.

(a legend of ancient Britain adapted from William of Malmesbury and other sources)

The Spider's Web

Luke 2:41-52

When wise men from the East travelled many miles to see the new baby Jesus, they first visited King Herod, to find out from him where the baby had been born. Herod was furious — and frightened. He didn't want to lose his throne to a new prince, so he ordered the Imperial Guard to search out and murder all baby boys under two years old.

While Joseph was dreaming, he was warned by an angel to flee from Bethlehem, under cover of night. Quickly he woke Mary. She scooped up baby Jesus in her arms, making sure he was snug and warm, then they gathered their few belongings together, fetched the donkey, and set off on their long trek across the desert.

The night air grew colder. All the small creatures of the desert were concerned for the young family. Night beetles glowed in the dark, to help show the way. Bats flitted across the dark sky, to keep them company. But the way was long and hard. Many times Mary and Joseph stumbled, and Mary grew more and more tired. Eventually they decided to rest, and crept inside a dank cave on the hillside, a few miles outside Bethlehem.

A tiny spider who lived at the entrance to the cave was thrilled that the Holy Family had come to shelter in his cave. He wanted so much to help the new baby, to give him some sort of present, but he didn't know what to give. Then he had a brainwave. He decided to spin an enormous web, bigger than anything he'd ever attempted before, to fill the entrance to the cave. That might, he thought, keep out some of the cold air, so that the baby would be just a little warmer.

It was a huge job for such a tiny spider, but he set to work with a will and toiled all night, spinning and weaving, weaving and spinning. As dawn broke, the tiny spider collapsed, exhausted. But his work was done. The mouth of the cave was completely filled with the spider's web.

Just then came the noise of horses' hooves thudding along the ground and the cry of soldiers. "Over here, Captain," shouted one of the soldiers. "There's a cave here. Perhaps they're hiding inside the cave." All the little creatures of the desert held their breath as the soldiers rushed over to the cave. The tiny spider sat in his web, not daring to move. Then the Captain said: "You fool! Nobody's been in this cave for years! Look at that web. Anyone can see it's been there ages. We'll not waste our time looking in this cave."

As the soldiers rode away, the tiny spider breathed a great sigh of relief. His web had saved the day! Just then the baby looked up at the spider and chuckled, and the web shone in the light of the baby's smile.

That is why, from that day to this, if you see a spider's web early on a cold morning, you'll find it glistens and gleams. And that's why we put tinsel on the Christmas tree — to remind us of the day the tiny spider saved the life of the Holy Family.

(adapted from an ancient legend)

The Fiery Princess

Luke 3:15-17, 21-22

John the Baptist told his followers that the Messiah (Jesus) would baptise with fire. But fire can be dangerous; people can get burnt if fire is not controlled and channelled. This is a story about a young princess with a fiery temper, who only found happiness when her temper was properly controlled.

Once upon a time there lived a king and a queen in the most beautiful kingdom in the whole wide world. The king and queen were good people, and were greatly loved by all their subjects, so the kingdom, as well as being beautiful, was a very happy place. When a tiny princess was born to the king and queen, the whole kingdom rejoiced. People came from far and near to peep at the new baby, who lay in her little cradle and cooed and chuckled at all her visitors. Everybody agreed she was the most adorable baby they'd ever seen.

When she was very hungry or very tired, little Princess Serena would screw up her tiny face, open her tiny mouth, and emit the loudest of screams. People in the farthest corners of the kingdom always heard her. They'd smile tolerantly and nod their heads wisely and say to each other: "Serena's hungry again. Isn't it good to have a princess who makes her presence felt."

Serena grew into the prettiest little girl anyone had ever seen. Like all storytime princesses, she had golden curls and deep blue eyes, a dimpled chin and a gorgeous smile, so that everybody loved her. She was nearly perfect. Nearly, but not quite, for Serena had just one problem. When she was displeased or unhappy, Serena would immediately have a tantrum. She'd flare up over the slightest thing. Her face would go bright red, she'd screw up her eyes and her mouth, and scream.

As she grew older, people in the farthest corners of the kingdom stopped saying it was good to have a princess who made her presence felt, and began to say: "There's that Serena again. Just listen to the noise she makes. I wish we could move away from this kingdom to somewhere out of earshot." One day, when Serena was a teenager, her mother the queen mildly remarked: "Serena, I wish you'd tidy your bedroom. It's such a mess."

With that, the princess erupted. She shouted and screamed and stamped and roared. She completely lost her temper. But sadly, once lost, she was unable to find her temper again. The king ordered a search of the palace. The people who worked in the palace looked everywhere. They searched under beds and in cupboards. They peered into nooks and crannies. They rummaged through drawers and cabinets. But there wasn't a sign of the princess's temper. The king extended the search into the palace grounds. People explored bushes and examined trees and hunted through the undergrowth. They probed the flower beds and investigated the stone ornaments and statues. They scoured every inch of the palace grounds, but to no avail. Serena's temper was nowhere to be seen.

At last the king called the princess. "My dear," he said kindly, "I fear the only person who can find your temper is you yourself. Take this horse, the best we have in the palace stables, and ride out into the kingdom. When you find your temper again, come back to us so that we may all rejoice."

Furiously, Princess Serena snatched the reins from her father's hands. Leaping into the saddle she galloped off into the night with an angry snarl. For many months she rode the length and breadth of the kingdom searching for her temper. But whenever she knocked on doors to inquire whether anyone had seen her temper, the doors remained firmly closed. People were afraid of a person who was permanently angry and refused to have anything to do with the princess. Sometimes Serena spotted a curtain twitching, and then she'd scream at the house, calling the occupants utter fools, and threatening to come back and show them what for, if they didn't open the door. But it made no difference. Nobody wanted to know the princess.

Eventually, Serena found herself in a dark and gloomy wood. It perfectly matched her mood, for people who are permanently angry are also permanently unhappy. Serena rode through the wood, muttering blackly to herself and pulling branches off the trees just because she felt like it, when suddenly she came upon an old and dilapidated cottage.

She banged on the cottage door and shrieked at the top of her voice: "Open up! I want to talk to you. Now."

To her great surprise, the door opened. A very old and bent man stood there, smiling at her.

Serena was astounded. She hadn't seen a smile for years. "I'm coming in," she bellowed at the old man.

He opened the door wider, and grinned a toothless grin, for he was too old to have any teeth. Serena went into the cottage, sat herself down, and began to shout at the old man.

He responded with delight. Then he made some tea and some sandwiches, and they sat there all afternoon, eating and drinking. Serena was mystified. "Why aren't you afraid of my shouting?" she asked. "Everyone is terrified of me. They all close their doors immediately when they see me coming."

"Shouting?" said the old man. "My dear, I can only just hear you. It's a joy to me to have someone who speaks up so clearly. My old ears don't hear too well."

"But don't you know who I am?" pressed Serena. "Nobody likes me. I've never been invited to tea before."

"My old eyes don't see too clearly," said the old man. "I like you just as you are."

Then Serena asked the old man if he'd seen her temper, or knew where it was, for she'd lost it many months before and had never found it again.

The old man looked astonished. "My dear," he said, "I think if you look inside yourself, you'll see you've already found your temper. And if you know where it's kept, you need never lose it again. But should you ever want to visit me again, I'm always here, in my little house in the woods."

Serena looked inside herself and realised she was happy for the first time in years. She was so delighted to have her temper back that she gave the old man a big hug. She rode back to the palace full of smiles. From that day onward people used to say: "Princess Serena. How her name suits her, for she's the most serene person we've ever met." And do you know, Serena never lost her temper again. But try as she might, neither did she ever find that little house in the woods again.

The Reluctant Bridesmaid

John 2:1-11

When Jesus visited a wedding at Cana in Galilee, he showed that human disappointments matter to him and that he would be prepared to redeem them. This is a story about a young girl's bitter disappointment when she became a bridesmaid.

Seven-year-old Claire Philips was jumping up and down in excitement. A letter had arrived that morning from a distant cousin, who was to be married in two month's time. The letter was to invite Claire to be a bridesmaid. Claire had never been a bridesmaid before, but she'd always longed to be one. She'd been to three weddings and each time had envied the young bridesmaids in their beautiful dresses and shining hairstyles.

Every night when Claire said her prayers before settling down to sleep, she prayed for the chance to be a bridesmaid. And now here it was! On March 23rd, Claire would become a bridesmaid herself. She circled the date on the kitchen calendar with red biro, and each evening crossed another day off, so that she knew exactly how many days were left.

One day, the distant cousin arrived and whisked Claire off to the dressmaker. Her bridesmaid's dress was to be a long dress made out of green velvet, and Claire thought she'd never seen anything so beautiful. The material was so lovely to touch that Claire could have stayed there all day, just stroking the velvet. She was measured and pinned and stood on chairs and fussed over until she felt quite tired. But it was that lovely, warm comfortable sort of tiredness that comes when you're really happy.

On the great day, Claire had to get up very early. Her parents drove her a long way to the distant cousin's house, and as soon as they arrived, Claire was hustled indoors.

The house was in chaos. There were two other big bridesmaids there, both worrying about spots on their faces, although Claire couldn't see any. The bride herself seemed to be in a funny kind of dream, drifting from one room to another. The bride's mother was fretting over everyone and everything. The bride's father, for some reason Claire couldn't make out, looked terrified and disappeared into a tiny room at the top of the house.

Very soon a hairdresser arrived, and Claire found her hair being washed and curled, styled with some tiny white rosebuds, and sprayed with some nasty sticky stuff that made Claire choke and made her hair feel all stiff, like a piece of cardboard. But when she looked in the mirror, she could hardly recognise herself, she looked so glamorous. Then somebody helped her into the dress, and she put on some shoes with a little heel, which felt terribly wobbly when she walked. So she sat down quietly in a corner until the photographer appeared. Someone handed her a little basket of flowers, which she had to hold in all sorts of strange positions while the photographer took pictures. Claire thought the pictures might go on forever, he took so many, but at last he was finished.

Then a big car arrived, which took the three bridesmaids and the bride's mother to the church. They had to wait for a while in the church porch, while the car went back for the bride and her father. The wait made Claire feel quite cold, and she wished they'd hurry up. But eventually the bride arrived, they all moved into position behind her and her father, and the church organ struck up some loud and glorious special wedding music. This was it, the greatest moment of Claire's life! The church was full, and everyone turned to look as the procession began its slow glide down the aisle. From all round, there were tiny gasps of appreciation and little murmurs of delight.

But to her horror, Claire discovered it was very difficult to walk in the unfamiliar shoes. She tottered a bit and put out her hand to steady herself. She tried to smile as she'd been told. But it was hopeless. To her dismay, Claire found herself staggering and swaying, wobbling and tottering. She was used to running about in trainers, and she found it almost impossible to walk so slowly on the little heels. Then, after one particularly bad wobble, when she nearly fell, out of the corner of her eye Claire noticed a lady in the congregation smiling. The smile grew to a chuckle and the chuckle seemed to spread from one to another until it seemed to Claire as if every single person in the entire church was looking at her and roaring with laughter. Claire was so ashamed. She felt herself grow bright red, and her lip began to tremble. She knew she was going to cry.

Suddenly, she hated being a bridesmaid. Suddenly, it had all gone wrong. She longed to be at home, away from this horrible church and silly dress and stupid shoes. But most of all, she wanted her Mum. How she longed for her Mum, but she had no idea where her parents had gone when they'd dropped her at the bride's house. She assumed they'd probably gone home, she hadn't thought to ask.

She looked down at the floor and bit her lip, but the first tear escaped and ran down her face onto the green velvet, where it settled with a little mark. Claire felt desperate. They were nearly at the top of the aisle now, but she was terrified she might fall at any time. Or that she'd ruin the dress with her tears. She said a quick prayer: "Please God, help me!"

Then she risked a glance around. And to her astonishment and delight she saw her Mum and Dad, nearly in the front row. Her Mum smiled at her and winked, and looked so pleased and proud. Claire suddenly realised nobody was laughing any more. And miraculously, she was walking straight without a single wobble!

The tears dried up. Claire looked at her Mum and smiled. It had been so nearly a disaster, but somehow she knew everything would be all right now. She knew she was going to love being a bridesmaid whatever happened, and she knew it was going to be the best day of her life after all.

Oscar's Courage

Luke 4:14-21

> *When Jesus chose that particular passage from Isaiah, he went to the heart of his gospel — an option for the poor. But the existence of large numbers of poor keep comfortable people comfortable, so he was immediately marked out as a dangerous person with dangerous ideas. And he was eventually executed for his beliefs.*
>
> *Today's story is about Oscar Romero, who suffered a similar fate when he too chose an option for the poor.*
>
> *The Christian gospel is a dangerous gospel when its truth is really heard.*
>
> *(All the information for this story is from the website for The Nuclear Age Peace Foundation: www.wagingpeace.org.)*

About twenty years ago, a young priest was shot and killed on the streets of El Salvador. His "crime" was to speak out against the government, for many people in El Salvador had been executed by death squads, and many more had simply disappeared, and were never heard of again. The priest, Father Grande, denounced these death squads and the terrible cruelty encouraged by the government. People were very poor and lived in great fear, for nobody knew who would be executed next. Father Grande preached the Christian gospel of love for everybody, and said the government was wrong in the way it treated the people. And so he was shot.

Father Grande's great friend, bishop Oscar Romero, had just been appointed Archbishop in El Salvadore. There were two types of church people in El Salvadore at the time. Those like Father Grande, who spoke out against the government, and those who kept quiet, who tried not to upset the government, so that no one else would be killed. Bishop Oscar was chosen to be archbishop because the authorities thought he was one of those who would keep quiet.

But Archbishop Oscar changed after his friend's death. He was so angry and upset at the way his friend had been killed just because he preached the gospel, that he too began to speak against the government. He saw the poverty and injustice and sorrow of the people and was determined to make the Church a beacon of hope and light for the people.

And so Archbishop Oscar became a defender of the poor and began to denounce from the pulpit the evils of state-supported death squads. As a gesture of solidarity with the preachings of Father Grande, Archbishop Oscar refused to appear in any public ceremonies with any army or government personnel until the true nature of his friend's murder was brought out and true social change began. Never before had such a high-ranking church leader made such a bold move.

Archbishop Oscar soon became the voice and conscience of El Salvador. His words and actions were heard throughout the whole world, so that soon, everybody knew what was happening in El Salvador. Archbishop Oscar's fight for human rights led to his nomination for the Nobel Peace Prize. He spoke words of peace, but they were a threat to the government, for when the whole world is watching, it's harder to terrorise, torture, and murder.

On March 24, 1980 at 6:25 p.m. Archbishop Oscar was leading a communion service. As he prepared the Eucharist, a shot from the back of the church struck him in the chest, killing him instantly. So Archbishop Oscar died for the gospel of Christ, but his words, deeds, and actions remained very much alive.

Today El Salvador remains a country of misery and injustice. Yet Oscar Romero's spirit lives on and his teachings remain. Let us remember him and continue to strive for the realisation of his gospel dream: truth, justice, dignity, and human rights for all the people of the world.

Anna's Story

Luke 2:22-40

> *The story of the presentation of Jesus in the temple is strong on two "bit-part" characters, Simeon and Anna, both of whom are old, and neither of whom has any other mention in the Bible. This story is an imaginary biography of Anna.*

My name is Anna. I'm a very old lady now. I think at my next birthday I shall probably be 85, although I'm not sure exactly when I was born. My life now is very quiet. I spend most of my day and night at the temple, and when I'm able, I even sleep in the Courtyard of Women. Sometimes the guards throw me out and I sleep huddled up against the outer walls of the temple, but mostly they're very kind and allow me to melt into the shadows. I guess it's because I've been here so long.

I remember so well the day I came. I was only young. I was married at the age of thirteen or fourteen, I can't quite remember exactly, to Elias. He was a good man, of the tribe of Reuben. Much older than me, of course, but my father Phanuel took great care to choose a man who was kind and considerate, and who would look after me properly. My father was very advanced in his thinking. He always showed me love and affection, and even allowed me a little education. I learned as a child to read our scriptures, although I could seldom get my hands on a scroll. Mostly they were locked away by the priests. Elias encouraged my reading, and sometimes we would read and praise God together.

I wanted so much to give Elias a child, but it wasn't to be. He had no children by his first wife, and as I was young and healthy, it never occurred to me I might have difficulty conceiving. But it wasn't to be, and it seemed God had put his curse on me, for after seven short years of marriage, my beloved Elias suddenly died.

I shall never forget that time. The shock of those cousins of his running into our house and telling me he was dead. I was only twenty years old and already a widow. I remember so well the wailing of the other women and the weeks of mourning. And through it all I was numb, unable to feel. It was as though it was happening to somebody else. Even when the period of mourning was over, I still felt dazed and unreal. And I didn't know what to do. Elias had no brothers who could marry me, and I couldn't return to the tribe of Asher, for I was no longer a young virgin but a mature married woman.

In my hour of need I turned to God. I went to the temple and railed at God. I wept and screamed and beat my breast. I put on sackcloth and poured ashes on my head, but to no avail. God was silent. He never responded.

I think, staying there day after day weeping and crying, I scared the temple authorities at that time, for they kept their distance and mostly tolerated my presence. Perhaps they thought I was mad and they were afraid of the demons within me.

As the years passed, I gradually became calmer. Perhaps it was the atmosphere of the temple, God's house. I kept my ears to the ground and picked up every smidgen of gossip. Once I heard that the Day of the Lord was growing closer. I can't describe the wild excitement that filled me when I heard that. Without knowing what I was doing, I opened my mouth to praise God and strange words poured out. I had no idea what I was saying, the words came from deep within me and I was powerless to prevent their escape. The people standing by were startled, and soon quite a crowd had gathered. One man in the crowd cried out: "She's prophesying! Her words come from God!" And after that I was treated with considerable veneration. It happened again and again, this strange prophecy, and I had no control over it. I would simply open my mouth, and the words poured out. I began to wonder whether this was the reason God had kept me barren and caused me so much pain, so that I could prophesy for him.

Now and again Simeon would come into the temple. I'd known Simeon most of my life, we were children together. I think perhaps he came to keep an eye on me, to make sure I was all right. He came one day while I was prophesying. When I'd finished, he seemed to be bathed in a clear white light. His face shone, and he looked up to heaven and spoke the most beautiful words. He said God had given him the interpretation of my words, and that the promised Messiah would soon be amongst us. And he also said that neither he nor I would die until we had seen the Messiah for ourselves. I laughed at him. Who were we to meet the promised Messiah? Everybody knew he wouldn't come to ordinary people like us! But I was secretly excited by Simeon's words.

After that, I waited and watched every day to see the Messiah, but he never came. I've grown old waiting, and so has Simeon. I think I've spent most of my life waiting for God, but he's never come, and he's never given me what I wanted. I wanted a child, he made me a prophetess. I wanted a home, he made me live in the temple. I wanted happiness, he gave me patience. I wanted words of comfort, he gave me silence.

But today! Somehow today is special. I feel it in my old bones. The very stones of the temple seem to be singing a secret song. There's an air of excitement and expectancy, and dear old Simeon has just come in. I know he feels it too. He hasn't glanced in my direction, but I can feel his mood. Something is going to happen. Could this be the day?

A shabby little family has just come in. They don't have much money, they have only the lesser sacrifice of a couple of turtledoves. But wait! There's something very special about this family. This is it! This is it! I know it, deep within me. I can feel the words rising in my breast, praise God! Praise God, for this is his Messiah! This tiny baby, who has just given me the most beautiful smile — he knows who I am! This baby knows me!

Old Simeon is interpreting my words: "Lord, now lettest thou thy servant depart in peace, according to thy word; for mine eyes have seen the salvation that thou has prepared in the presence of all peoples, a light for revelation to the Gentiles and for glory to thy people Israel."

To God be the glory! He has given us a Son to redeem Jerusalem! Now indeed Simeon and I can depart in peace, for we have lived for this moment.

Martin's Story

Luke 5:1-11

The disciples may not have understood or agreed with Jesus' instructions to lower their nets on the other side of the boat. But they complied, nevertheless, and hauled in a huge catch of fish, way beyond their wildest dreams.

This is a story about Martin's difficulty in building a church from a matchstick kit, until he followed the advice and directions of someone who was wiser and more experienced in model-making than he was.

"It's the perfect solution," thought Martin as he ran up the stairs to the loft. "Gran's always been interested in things I've made, and she loves her church, so it should be the ideal present."

He rummaged about in one of the old boxes thrown into a corner in the loft. Every so often, Martin's mother had what she called "a good clear-out," which meant a number of Martin's older toys would disappear from his room, never to be seen again. Not that he minded. His Mum always checked with him first, and only cleared out the things he'd outgrown.

He'd been given the kit a couple of Christmases ago, although his brother James was the acknowledged model-maker in the family. Martin had been quite intrigued at the time and had taken a good look at both the outside of the box and its contents. He'd even pulled out the instruction leaflet and given it a quick glance, but it had looked so complicated he'd put the kit to one side and had conveniently forgotten all about it. His Mum had left it lying on the floor of his room for a year before she'd carted it upstairs with a lot of other junk and the usual tutting noise, which Martin always ignored.

He'd remembered the kit while he was racking his brains for a birthday present for his Gran. He'd been unable to think beyond chocolates, when a picture of the kit popped into his mind. It was inspired! The perfect gift, and he knew his Gran would love it because he'd have made it himself.

Martin dusted the box with the sleeve of his sweatshirt and peered at the picture. It looked easier than he remembered, quite a simple church with some stained glass windows and a spire. Of course, he was two years older now, so something that had seemed fiendishly difficult then would probably be child's play now. Anyway, if James could make things, so could he.

Martin tipped out the contents of the box onto the kitchen table, taking care to keep each matchstick in its correct group. There were hundreds of matchsticks of varying lengths, but all quite small. It looked as if it was going to be a fiddly job, and for a moment Martin felt a little daunted.

Then he reminded himself he was doing it not for himself, but for his Gran, and felt better. He poked about in the kitchen drawer for some of his brother's modelling glue, and sat down to study in detail the picture on the box. The instructions had long since disappeared, probably thrown out with the Christmas wrapping paper two years ago, but Martin didn't think it would matter too much. All he had to do was follow the picture.

The project started quite well. Martin even remembered to cover the kitchen table with newspaper, just in case. He studied the picture carefully, then started with the base of the church and began to build up the walls, carefully gluing each matchstick in place. It was a little tricky round the door, but he managed to sort it out.

The problems began with the windows and the spire. Try as he would, he couldn't get the matchsticks to fit. Either they were too long, or too short, or he needed a curve and couldn't make one. Martin could feel himself growing angrier by the minute. Stupid kit! Why couldn't they make it easy, like it looked on the box?

When his brother came in, took one look and started to laugh, Martin wanted to burst into tears or throw the kit across the room. Of course he didn't do either. He jumped up and punched his brother instead. James fended him off and said tolerantly, "You need to start with the spire. Build that first, and everything else'll fit."

"Think you're so clever, just because you've made a few model cars," retorted Martin. "What d'you know about buildings? Nothing! Anyway, this isn't plastic like your silly cars, it's real wood and it's delicate work."

James roared with laughter and shrugged. "Suit yourself," he said, "I'm off to play football."

"Good riddance," snarled Martin, and slammed the door after his know-it-all brother.

Then Martin made himself a drink and went in to watch some television. He felt fed up and miserable and angry and wished someone would come and help him.

When the programme finished, Martin went back to his model. He couldn't think how to tackle it, so decided to try the spire, if only to prove James wrong. He started to glue the matchsticks together, and found they fitted quite well. This was better. Martin began to hum to himself as the spire grew and took shape. He became so absorbed in his task, he didn't notice the hours passing.

When the spire was complete, Martin sat back and looked at it. It was perfect! An exact miniature replica of their own church spire. Eagerly, he returned to the rest of the model, and before long the church began to fit snugly to the spire. He left the windows until last, and covered them with some tiny pieces of coloured cellophane, to look like glass.

At last he was finished, and he was delighted with his work. It looked better than he could ever have imagined. He knew his Gran would be thrilled, although actually, he felt so proud of his achievement, it would be a wrench now to part with his church.

James came in from football and peered carefully at the finished church. Then he nodded approvingly.

"Told you so," he said.

I Want to Be

Luke 6:17-26

We tend to think of Saints as special holy people who are perhaps not quite real. But in this reading, Jesus makes it clear that those who are very ordinary because they are poor, hungry, sad, or otherwise disadvantaged in some way, are especially blessed. This is a story about Casper, who spoke in fun but found his words were taken rather seriously.

Casper's aunt was visiting. It was always a pain, because she always asked him the same things, one of which was, "What do you want to be when you're grown up, Casper?" Since Casper didn't want to grow up at all, the question was meaningless. But up it came, year after year, and Casper was always forced to mumble some unsatisfactory reply. But this year, Casper had his answer ready.

"What do you want to be when you grow up, Casper?" asked his aunt, in that bright tone of voice she used when talking to children.

Casper beamed at her and adopted his most innocent expression. "A saint," he said.

There was a moment's shocked hush, then Casper's father burst out laughing. But his aunt's face lost its brightness and her mouth turned down at the corners. It was clear she couldn't think of anything to say. Casper was well pleased and went out to play.

That night as he lay sleeping, Casper was suddenly woken by a bright light shining on his face. He struggled up in bed. Standing in front of him and filling his room was an angel. "You called me," the angel said to Casper.

Casper gulped. "I didn't!"

The angel nodded. "You said you wanted to be a saint. Here I am, to help you."

"But I didn't mean it," protested Casper.

"Too late," said the angel. "You spoke the words. They can't be un-spoken." He sat himself comfortably on Casper's bed. "Where shall we start? Shall I tell you about saints of the past?"

"Look," said Casper hurriedly, feeling this was all getting out of hand far too quickly. "I'm not the saintly type. I'm not good. You should see me at school, I'm the worst in the class. The teachers hate me."

"Good," said the angel, nodding. "Blessed are those who are hated and reviled. St. Augustine was like you. A really wild one, he was. We almost despaired of him. But his Mum kept on praying for him, and he eventually saw the light. There was no stopping him then. If it wasn't for St. Augustine, your church wouldn't be here today."

"That's where you're wrong," said Casper with some satisfaction. "I happen to know who brought Christianity to East Anglia, and it wasn't St. Augustine. It was St. Fursey."

"Who?" The angel wrinkled his brow. "Oh, him! Yes, he was a very early missionary. He came from Ireland to Burgh Castle and founded a monastery within the walls of the Roman fort on the banks of the River Waveney. But what about Felix? You'd have liked him. He came to East Anglia in 631 at about the same time as Fursey, but he was a bishop. He stayed for seventeen years and built a school here."

Casper made a face. He wasn't at all sure he would have liked some-one who started schools. He changed the subject. "Why are all the saints men?" he asked.

"They're not," replied the angel. "St. Julian of Norwich was a wom-an who had sixteen visions when she was thirty, and spent the next twenty years living in a tiny cell, meditating on those visions. You can still read what she discovered."

Casper sighed. "You see? I don't want to do *anything* like that! I want life to be fun and exciting. Saints are so boring. They don't do anything exciting."

"But they do," countered the angel, flapping his wings a little to ease the stiffness in them. There wasn't room to spread them in Casper's bedroom. "How about St. George, patron saint of England? He was a knight in shining armour, who killed a terrible fire-breathing dragon to save the people. And Joan of Arc? She was burned at the stake because she stood up for her beliefs. That exciting enough for you? Or how about St. Stylites? He was a little odd, I must admit. He spent his life living on top of a pole."

Casper wasn't entirely happy about the direction of the conversation. Fighting dragons was okay, but he had no wish to be burned at the stake. And living on top of a *pole*? "Anyway," he said, "I'm only ordinary, so I'll never be a saint."

Then the angel beamed. "That's really what I've come to tell you. When the Christian Church first started, all Christians were known as 'saints.' That was the name for them. If you just grow up being yourself and hanging onto to Jesus with all your might, you'll be a saint too. That's the secret of all the saints, the ones you know and all those many saints you've never heard of. Why, if you look around your church congregation, you'll probably find quite a number of saints. But they won't know they're saints and most other people won't recognise it either. But those who are hungry for God are especially blessed, and those who are really sad now will find themselves laughing."

"You mean," asked Casper carefully, "I can just be myself, not specially good or anything, and as long as I keep holding onto God and feeling hungry for him for all I'm worth, I could become a saint and no one need ever know? And I won't necessarily die some horrible death? Or have to do something really stupid like that Style bloke?"

The angel nodded.

"Oh well," said Casper. "That's all right then." And he turned over and went back to sleep.

Princess Lightfinger

Luke 8:22-25

*This is a story about a princess who finds herself in terrible trouble.
She thinks nobody cares about her or her problems, but in the end,
the storm calms and she realises how much she's always been loved.*

When Princess Lightfinger was born, there was great rejoicing in the whole land. Sticking firmly to the old traditions, the king and queen chose the best possible fairy godmother for their daughter, a fairy godmother who would look after the princess at all times, and who would always have the princess' best interests at heart.

As the princess grew up, she developed a warm and loving relationship with her fairy godmother. If ever she was in trouble, Princess Lightfinger would turn to her fairy godmother, who would always listen patiently and never scolded the princess.

Being a princess, Lightfinger had almost everything she wanted. She had beautiful clothes, all the latest CDs and video games, and a lot of pocket money every week. But there was something she wanted, which she couldn't have.

The woodcutter's daughter, who lived in a tiny cottage in the palace grounds, and who was about the same age as the princess, had a new puppy. The puppy was gorgeous, small and cute and fluffy. And it was full of fun. When the woodcutter's daughter threw a ball, the puppy would race after it, bring it back, and drop it to be thrown again. And when the woodcutter's daughter held up a biscuit, the puppy would sit on its hind legs and beg and even shake hands with the girl. The woodcutter's daughter was so happy with her new puppy, she played with him all day long.

Princess Lightfinger longed for a puppy of her very own. Although she was a princess, she was quite lonely, because she wasn't allowed to play with children who weren't royal, and there weren't many other princes or princesses around.

She begged the king and queen for a puppy, but they were adamant. "Sorry, Lightfinger," said the king. "We go away too often on state business. It wouldn't be fair to have a puppy and then just leave it for somebody else to look after." And however much Lightfinger pouted and sulked, shouted and stamped, the king wouldn't give in.

Lightfinger took to wandering down to the woodcutter's cottage and hiding behind one of the big trees, just to see the puppy. How she longed to pat him and cuddle him and take him out for a walk in the forest.

Then one day, the woodcutter's daughter was called in from the garden. She ran in through the door of the cottage, leaving the puppy romping on the front lawn. Before she knew what she was doing, Lightfinger had climbed the fence, run to the puppy, and thrown her arms around him. He licked her face and squirmed delightedly in her arms. In an instant, Lightfinger had picked him up and slipped out of the gate. Scarcely aware of herself, she ran down the track into the forest.

When she was well out of sight, Lightfinger set the puppy down and threw a pinecone for him. The puppy raced after the cone and brought it back, just as if it was a ball. Lightfinger had the best afternoon of her life, playing with the puppy.

When dusk began to fall, Lightfinger remembered the woodcutter's daughter and had a momentary twinge of guilt. Perhaps the girl was missing her puppy. Lightfinger picked up the pinecone for the final time, resolved to have one last throw and then take the puppy back. She threw the cone as hard as she could in amongst the trees. The puppy scampered after it — and didn't return.

Lightfinger called and called, but the puppy never came. The princess began to run into the trees, searching and calling, but there was no sign of the puppy. The princess shivered. It was cold now. Darkness had fallen, and she had no idea where she was. She'd never been this far into the forest before. She sat down on a log and started to cry.

How she wished she'd never taken the puppy! How she wished she'd never ventured alone into the forest! How she wished someone would come and help her! Then she began to think of what they'd say at home, and she sobbed even harder. Then she thought of how the woodcutter's daughter must be feeling. And the princess realised that if she ever got home again, she'd have to face the woodcutter's daughter. She felt sick. She who had everything had taken the only possession of the poor woodcutter's daughter, and now she'd lost that beloved puppy.

The princess wondered whether anyone would come looking for her. But there were no welcoming lights and no friendly voices, just the ghostly rustlings of small nighttime animals. It was getting rather scary.

Lightfinger began to realise nobody cared about her. They were probably all glad she was lost in the forest. It was a fitting punishment for her badness. She heaved a huge, sad sigh, then she said out loud: "O please, someone, help me!"

At once there was the whisper of a breeze in the air as fairy-light wings flitted through the darkness. Within seconds, Lightfinger's fairy godmother was there beside her. "Hush now, why are you crying?" asked her fairy godmother. "Did you think I didn't care? Did you think I'd stop loving you because you've been selfish and thoughtless? You only had to ask, and I'd be with you. Come now, let's get you home. Your mother and father are growing anxious about you."

They walked back through the forest together. When they reached the gate of the woodcutter's cottage, Lightfinger stopped. "I must go in and tell them about the puppy," she said, bravely. Her fairy godmother squeezed her hand. "I'll come with you."

As the door opened, something came hurtling out of the cottage and flung itself into Lightfinger's arms. A wet nose pushed into her face and a rough tongue began to lick her cheek. "You're home!" cried Lightfinger. "Oh, you're home! I'm so glad. And I'm so very sorry I took you."

"It's all right," said the woodcutter's daughter, smiling. "He knows his way home from the forest. He's been there hundreds of times and he likes you. You can come and take him out any time you want."

Lightfinger gasped in amazement. After all she'd done, and the awful way in which she'd treated her, the woodcutter's daughter had forgiven her already. Suddenly, the princess knew one thing for certain. However much she wanted it, she'd never take anything without permission ever again.

The Holy Grail

Luke 9:28-36

> *This is a story about a boy who is tormented by bullies, but his life is transformed when he makes a special discovery. He has to negotiate a dark and scary tunnel to make his discovery, but the discovery enables him to find inner strength and purpose, which he hadn't realised he possessed.*

Arthur ran along the beach to his favourite cave. He often went there when he was feeling sad or upset, and he always went alone. Months ago, he'd discovered the cave all by himself, and he'd never told anyone of its existence. It was his own special place, and despite the constant warnings about the dangers of high tides flooding caves, and rock falls blocking caves, Arthur felt safe there.

The kids from school had been at it again. This time they'd waylaid him on the way to school and had stolen his dinner money. Then they'd pushed him face down in the mud and torn his new blazer. When the school bell had rung and they'd at last disappeared, Arthur had taken off. He knew it would be even worse if he appeared in school with tear streaks down his muddy face, so he resolved to spend the day by himself in his cave.

He'd never spent a whole day there before, and it felt like a real adventure. Arthur's spirits lifted as he squeezed through the tiny gap between the two great rocks blocking the entrance. This time he thought he'd explore the whole cave, not just the opening part. This time he'd go right into the darkness and down that tunnel he'd discovered.

Arthur felt his way cautiously around the wall of the cave. He switched on his torch to locate the entrance to the tunnel and felt in his pockets for something to mark his way, just in case there was a labyrinth of tunnels and he got lost. That packet of crisps the bullies had stamped into inedible crumbs would be ideal. Arthur opened the packet and dropped a little pile of crisp crumbs onto the floor. They were easy to see in the light of the torch, and it was a large packet so they should last.

He crept slowly into the tunnel, his heart beating very fast. It was pitch black and really scary, but he kept one hand on the wall and the other firmly clutching his torch. The roof was very low in parts, and for once Arthur was glad he was small and thin.

After several hundred yards, the tunnel widened out into a large amphitheatre. Arthur gasped. There was a shaft of sunlight filtering in from somewhere high up, so he could see reasonably well. This new cave had a little stream meandering along the bottom, and stalagmites and stalactites grouped at various bends along the stream. At one point the stalactites met the stalagmites and formed huge pillars reaching from the floor of the cave to the roof, and they glistened and shone in the sunlight.

It was like fairyland, and Arthur had it all to himself. He spent the day happily exploring and discovered he could easily climb out of the cave onto the cliff top if he followed the shaft of sunlight. He emerged into a little bushy copse and marked the exit so he could come and go at will.

When it began to grow late, near the time he ought to be home from school, Arthur slipped back into the cave for one last look. He shone his torch around, to fill his mind with memories that would sustain him until his next visit. Suddenly, something gleamed oddly in the beam of the torch. Arthur scrambled down for a better look.

There, wedged between a couple of rocks, was a silver cup. Gently, Arthur eased it out, trying hard not to scratch it. Although it was mostly dirty, Arthur could see the cup was beautiful, covered in ornate engravings. Arthur rubbed it on his sleeve half expecting a genie to appear and peered at it more closely. He knew immediately what it was, for he saw a similar silver cup used in church each week. But how had a silver chalice come to be in the cave, and how long had it been there?

Carefully, Arthur wrapped the chalice inside his blazer and took it home, resolved to clean it until it shone again. As he walked, he remembered the bullies and wondered whether he should take a long detour to avoid them, but strangely, he felt much more confident with the cup in his hands, and he walked with his head held high.

The bullies were waiting on the corner of his street, as he'd suspected they might be. But amazingly, Arthur didn't care. He didn't cross the road to avoid them, but walked purposefully straight through them, ignoring them. They were so taken aback they simply parted to let him through, somehow uneasily aware of his new confidence and inner strength. One or two half-heartedly called him names, but when that produced no reaction, they all slouched off, seeking better prey.

When his mother came home from work, Arthur had nearly finished cleaning the chalice. She admired it with him and listened quietly to his whole story. They decided together to call the police, for it was obvious the chalice had been stolen and dumped and was perhaps part of some larger haul.

The rest of the week was the best time Arthur had ever had. He made statements to the police, and before long newspaper journalists were interviewing him and taking his photo, which was on the front page of the next day's paper. After that, the local television studio rang up, and Arthur found himself on television. The council cleared away the rocks from the entrance to the cave and opened it up, and the television cameras took pictures of Arthur in the cave, Arthur discovering the chalice, Arthur showing the stalagmites and stalactites. He loved it. Especially as he was called a hero in all the papers.

A big haul of stolen church silver was discovered hidden in the cave and returned to the church authorities. The police arrested a gang of thieves whom they'd been tracking for months. The cave became a huge tourist attraction, for it turned out to be very old, and the stalagmites and stalactites were some of the best examples of their kind in the whole country.

After that, Arthur never had any more trouble with bullies. Everyone wanted to be his friend, and although his size didn't really alter, he never felt small and thin again. The chalice had to go back to its rightful home in a church far away, but Arthur didn't mind. Everyone else thought it was just an ordinary silver chalice that had been stolen, but deep inside himself Arthur knew it was really the Holy Grail lost and forgotten for centuries, for it had changed his life forever. Arthur the nerd, bullied and derided, was no more. In his place stood King Arthur, head of the Knights of the Round Table, discoverer of the Holy Grail.

The Big City

Luke 4:1-13

This is a story about some of the temptations and pressures facing vulnerable teenagers in today's society.

When Tracy was going on fifteen, her family decided to move to the city from the sleepy market town where Tracy had lived all her life. Tracy was so excited she could hardly wait. Nothing ever happened in the country. There was nothing to do, and along with all her friends, Tracy was usually bored. But things were so different in the city. There were cinemas and pubs and clubs. There was dancing and rock bands and bowling alleys. And there were buses! No longer would Tracy have to be transported by her parents anywhere she went and have to be picked up by them at some ridiculously early hour. Now she could be independent, and hopefully stay out much later.

Settling into her new school was a little more difficult than Tracy had anticipated. She felt diffident and strange amongst so many new faces and responded gratefully when anybody spoke to her. But they all talked about people and situations that were quite unknown to Tracy, and she felt very isolated and lonely.

A little group of girls made an effort to befriend her, and Tracy was glad enough to hang around with them. She soon became aware they were regarded as "sad" by the rest of the school, and she longed more than anything to be accepted by the "in" crowd, to be one of the popular people.

Everything changed six months later on Valentine's Day. Tracy arrived at school to discover a single red rose on her desk. She felt a tremendous excitement rising within her and blushed crimson. Everybody crowded round her desk, with exclamations of admiration and congratulations and hundreds of wild guesses as to the identity of the unknown sender. For once, Tracy found herself the centre of attention. Everybody wanted to be with her, everybody wanted to be her friend.

After school, instead of walking quickly home by herself as she usually did, Tracy meandered slowly homeward, surrounded by a group of
seven or eight youngsters, laughing and joking and teasing, and including her as one of themselves. Tracy walked on air. Not only had she
suddenly found friends, but she also had an unknown admirer who was
in love with her!

By the next day, the whole school knew the identity of Tracy's ro-
mantic admirer. He was Jamie Boulter, heart throb of year 10, streetwise,
rebellious, and daring. Tracy was thrilled. From that moment her life
changed. As Jamie's girlfriend, she became an accepted member of his
gang. He took her to all those places she'd dreamed of visiting. They went
to clubs and pubs, to the cinema, the bowling alley and the rock concerts.

Tracy learned to drink and smoke, and she learned to suck pepper-
mints before she went home, to disguise the smell of her breath. When
her parents asked her about the terrible smell of stale cigarette smoke on
her clothes, she admitted going to a pub, but denied smoking or drinking alcohol. "I only drank Coke," she said.

It felt so good to be part of the gang. Tracy was full of a new confidence and bravado. She was aware of a slight twinge of conscience when,
with the gang, she sneered at the sad people who had at first befriended
her, but she soon pushed her conscience to one side.

In the summer, she went with her new friends to the local park,
where they shared a spliff. Tracy had never tasted cannabis before and
voiced her unease at trying drugs, but when the gang teased her as being
Little Miss Self-Righteous, she too took a tentative drag. Jamie consoled
her on the way home. "You don't have to do anything you don't want,"
he assured her. "I won't let them get at you. If you don't want to smoke,
you needn't. I'll look after you."

Strangely enough, that re-inforced Tracy's desire to conform, and
she soon found she developed a taste for cannabis. And when the gang
had a discussion about soft drugs and agreed cannabis was safer than
tobacco and ought to be legalised, Tracy felt much better.

In one way, Tracy was enjoying herself more than she ever had before. She was discovering a new, reckless side to her nature, which was
very exciting. When she stopped to draw breath, she was amazed at her
own fearlessness. And yet, somewhere deep inside, she was somehow
anxious too. She was aware her parents were worried about her, but of

course they were so old they couldn't possibly understand. On one occasion she skipped a few lessons to go into the city with Jamie, and the
school rang her parents. There was a terrible scene at home, and Tracy
felt angry and hurt and upset all at the same time and refused to speak
to her parents for three whole days.

Things came to a head one Saturday. Tracy had gone into the city
with Jamie, who wanted to buy cigarettes at one of the local stores. They
met the gang in the city and wandered over to the shop together, laughing and jostling each other. Jamie told Tracy to wait outside the shop
and went inside with the others. Tracy felt a little forlorn, but she did as
she was told. She had an odd feeling about Jamie's activities inside the
shop, and she didn't really want to know what he was about.

She'd been waiting about ten minutes when a police car drew up silently at the kerb, and four police officers leapt out and ran into the shop.
Tracy thought her heart would burst, it was pumping so hard. She was
terrified. Images of newspaper headlines jumped into her mind, closely
followed by a picture of her parents, appalled and disbelieving. Without
thinking, she took to her heels and fled. She jumped on the nearest bus
and headed home to hide in her bedroom, hardly daring to breath.

Later, she rang Jamie, but there was no reply. She rang each of the
gang in turn but couldn't raise any of them. In school on the Monday,
she soon learned all the gang had been arrested for shoplifting. "It could
have been me," she thought to herself. "It nearly was! Thank God I
didn't go into that shop! Whatever has happened to me?"

Suddenly her new life didn't seem quite so sophisticated and glamorous. Suddenly it began to seem dirty and sordid and nasty. As Tracy
looked at herself, she found she didn't much like what she'd become.
She felt depressed and bad, and she hung her head to avoid catching
anyone's knowing glance.

To her astonishment, the sad people noticed her distress and instead
of jeering at her or telling her it served her right, they offered comfort
and friendship. They didn't ask any questions, but quietly and protec-
tively surrounded her, and fielded any probing comments. As Tracy
went with them, she began to realise they were offering much more
than Jamie and his gang had ever offered. And she thought perhaps she
might now like to get to know the sad people better. For suddenly, being
sad didn't seem to be quite such a terrible disaster.

Robert's Choice

Luke 13:31-35

> *Even after being warned that Herod was out to kill him, Jesus was still determined to go to Jerusalem. Was this his own free choice or was he propelled in some way? Did he choose to follow what he thought was God's will, or because he was both God and man, was his choice taken from him?*
>
> *This is a story about Robert, who felt he had no choice in a particular situation. The consequences of his actions were such that he realised we humans always have free will, and must exercise it responsibly.*

The four boys were dancing in a circle around Robert. They had their hands tucked under their armpits and were flapping their arms up and down like wings, and squawking and clucking like hens.

"Chicken! Chicken! Chicken!" they began to chant, until Robert felt tears begin to prickle behind his eyes.

"Shut up!" he shouted angrily. "I'm not chicken, I'm not! I'm not scared of anything."

But they only chanted all the louder, and whirled faster and faster until Robert wanted to cover his eyes and his ears with his hands.

"All right!" he shouted at last. "All right, I'll do it! But I think you're all mad and it's a stupid thing to do, so there!"

The boys grinned at each other and spread out on the kerb on either side of Robert.

"Here you go," said the biggest boy. "There's a car coming now. Not too soon, mind. It won't count if you go too soon."

Robert held his breath and prayed he wouldn't slip. He was relieved to see the car wasn't going too fast. When it was about fifteen metres away, he darted across the road. There was a slight screech of brakes, and he turned in time to see an angry face glaring at him, as the car shot past. Robert let out his breath in a long sigh and laughed with relief. His heart was hammering against his ribs, but it hadn't been as bad as he thought.

The other boys sauntered across the road. "Not bad for a first attempt," said one, and Robert felt a swell of pride. "No problem," he said jauntily. "It's no big deal. I can do it any time."

The five of them spent the rest of the afternoon playing chicken across the road, daring each other to leave it later and later before they ran. Robert felt exhilarated, really alive. This was fun! And he was just as good as any of the others.

He looked at his watch. Nearly tea time. "One last go," he called. And as he spotted a car in the distance, he added, "This one's mine!"

He was determined to make this the most exciting run ever. He waited and waited crouched ready for the dash, until he felt the tension of the other boys and heard them draw in their breath and the car was really close, then he tore across the road. He just made it! The car screeched loudly and swerved violently as the driver slammed on the brakes, and Robert laughed out loud. But a loud bang and a crash followed the screech, and Robert's laughter froze.

The car was crumpled silently against a lamppost. "Run!" hissed one of the boys, and Robert didn't wait for a second glance. He took to his heels. He didn't stop until he reached home. Nobody was in, so he switched on the television and sat in front of it. But he couldn't concentrate. He found he was shaking all over. All he could see was a blue car crumpled against a lamppost. He wondered about the driver and found himself praying the driver wasn't dead. He knew he should have stopped, or gone to offer first-aid like he'd been taught in the Cubs, and he felt deeply ashamed and very frightened.

It was ages before Robert's Mum came in, and when she did, she looked pale and worried. "What's the matter?" asked Robert, dread in his heart.

His Mum gave him a hug. "I don't want you to worry," she said, "but Gran's had a nasty accident in her car. She's in the hospital."

As Robert pictured his Gran's blue car, he felt as though an axe had hit him. "Can I see her?" he asked anxiously.

His Mum nodded. "We'll go tonight."

Robert's Gran had her leg strung up in a kind of sling, and a large bandage on her arm. There was a tube coming out of one hand, attached to a bottle of blood. She looked very pale and kind of old and frail but she managed a smile when she saw Robert and his Mum.

After a while, Robert's Mum went out to find a cup of tea. Robert sidled over to his Gran and held her hand tightly. He was nearly in tears.

His Gran began to speak, in a funny, croaky whisper. Robert had to put his ear close to her mouth to hear what she was saying. "Why did you do it, love?" she asked.

A tear escaped and rolled down Robert's cheek. "The others made me," he said miserably. "I didn't mean to hurt anyone, especially you. I never thought there'd be an accident."

"Robert," said his Gran, "nobody can make you do anything. You always have a choice. You could have chosen to let them laugh at you, and chosen not to play their silly games. God gave us free will, so we can always choose what we do. But we have to learn to choose responsibly." Then she winked at Robert and ruffled his hair with her free hand. "It takes more than that to kill off a tough old bird like me," she added, with a smile.

Robert threw his arms around her and hugged her. "You will be all right, won't you?" he asked.

Gran nodded. "I'll be out in a couple of days and raring to go."

Deep inside himself, Robert said a big thank you to God. Suddenly he knew he'd grown up a bit. For now he knew he'd never let anybody choose for him ever again.

The Worst Pixie in the World

Luke 13:1-9

In today's reading, Jesus showed that God's forgiveness is always available, although sometimes people are only brought to the point of forgiveness through difficulty and hardship — the manure around the fig tree. But Jesus also made it clear that bad things happen to everyone and are not a punishment from God.

This is a story about Clarrie, a very naughty pixie who bullied and intimidated the gentle fairy Delphinium. But when Clarrie tore her wing and was therefore grounded indefinitely, it was Delphinium who cared for her and showed her genuine forgiveness.

Clarrie was very angry. The Head Pixie had just informed her that a good fairy had been assigned to look after her. Clarrie didn't want anybody to look after her. She certainly didn't want some fairy, and she most definitely didn't want a fairy who was good.

Clarrie was *not* good. She worked hard at being bad, which was why the Head Pixie in despair, had turned to the fairies for help. Almost all fairies are good, and so are particularly suited to caring for others, even for bad pixies like Clarrie.

Clarrie's worst sins were hurting other pixies. She delighted in pinching pixie wings, or stamping hard on pixie toes, or hiding in the trees, then at night when it was dark and scary, jumping out with a loud shriek. All the other pixies were terrified of Clarrie and avoided her whenever they could. So Clarrie had no friends and was always alone.

That was the way she liked it. She couldn't be bothered with any of the other pixies, they were so boringly well-behaved. They never had any fun. Well, only feeble fun like playing games or flying sedately in a kind of pixie crocodile.

The Head Pixie had long despaired of Clarrie, but kept on forgiving her, hoping she'd perhaps become loveable one day. Clarrie regarded the Head Pixie with contempt. She considered the Head Pixie to be a total wimp, and every time the Head Pixie forgave her, Clarrie would immediately fly off and hatch a new plot even worse than previous schemes.

The crunch had finally come when Clarrie had torn a piece out of another pixie's wing. She hadn't actually meant to tear the wing, she'd only nailed it to a tree with a pine needle when the pixie was asleep. But the pixie had woken up with a start, and the wing had torn, and a little piece of wing was still nailed to the tree.

Pixie wings are very delicate. Any damage to a pixie wing is extremely painful, so the little pixie was in agony. Clarrie, whose wings had never been damaged, laughed out loud to see the little pixie's suffering. The Head Pixie had been horrified by Clarrie's lack of remorse and had resolved to call in the fairies. When Clarrie had begged and pleaded and implored forgiveness, the Head Pixie had stood firm and refused to budge.

It was a terrible disgrace to be put into the charge of a fairy. Clarrie didn't care about the disgrace, she rather enjoyed it and swaggered and boasted about how she was the worst pixie in the world. But when the good fairy Delphinium arrived, Clarrie's swagger changed to a depressed sort of limp, and her boasting became an angry moan.

The trouble with good fairies is, you can't get away from them. Delphinium stuck to Clarrie like glue. Clarrie had no opportunity for any mischief, because Delphinium was always there, like a kind of shadow.

Delphinium was so boring. For a start, she was always nice, no matter how rude Clarrie was to her. And she enjoyed fairy pursuits, like dancing in a ring and sitting on toadstools and helping whenever she could. All things Clarrie hated. Clarrie sat and sulked and tried to work out a way to shake off Delphinium.

She tried kicking and pinching and scratching and punching Delphinium, but the good fairy was quick and light and could fly out of trouble very fast indeed. Clarrie never got near enough to do any real damage. But she did say really nasty things to Delphinium and jeered and sneered at her so much that once or twice Clarrie noticed tears creep into Delphinium's blue eyes and her rosebud mouth droop in despondency.

One day, when Clarrie had shouted long and loud at Delphinium and told her how much she hated her, Delphinium turned her head away and closed her eyes for a moment. It was all the time Clarrie needed. Quick as lightning, she slipped the sharpest pine needle she could see into the palm of her hand. When Delphinium turned toward her again, Clarrie slashed at her face with the pine needle.

Delphinium screamed, a tiny, high fairy scream, and covered her face in her hands. Clarrie saw a drop of fairy blood ooze between Delphinium's fingers and with a sigh as soft as thistledown, Delphinium crumpled into a little fairy heap on the ground.

Clarrie gasped. She hadn't meant to hurt the fairy so much. She'd just wanted to frighten her. Suppose Delphinium was dead? She was lying very still. Clarrie took to her wings and started to fly as fast as her wings would carry her. But she was in such a hurry, she flew straight into a thorn bush. The last thing Clarrie remembered was the agonising pain in her wing as she caught it on a thorn and tore its delicate tissue.

When Clarrie came to, she was lying on a bed of soft moss, and somebody was gently bathing her injured wing in a soothing solution. As she struggled to sit up, Delphinium pushed her quietly back. "Hush now," whispered Delphinium. "You've hurt your wing quite badly. It'll heal in time, but I'm afraid there'll be no more flying for a while."

She looked so concerned and spoke in such a gentle voice that Clarrie stared at her. Eventually Clarrie said: "Don't you hate me? I've done such terrible things to you. Why don't you just leave me in pain? Why are you helping me?"

Delphinium laughed, a musical fairy laugh. "I don't hate you," she said. "I just want you to get better. And I'll help you all I can. I promise not to get in your way, and when you're really better, I'll ask the Head Pixie if you can be by yourself again. I know you don't really like having me around."

But to her surprise, Clarrie heard herself saying: "Don't go, please don't leave me. I wish you'd stay." Then she caught hold of Delphinium's hand and clasped it tightly. "I'm so sorry for all I've done to you and everyone else," she whispered. "I know you must hate me. I hate myself."

Delphinium simply put her arms around Clarrie and hugged her. "I'm your friend," she said. "I could never hate you."

Do you know, after that Clarrie changed so much she became the Best Pixie in the World, and everyone was her friend. She never hurt anybody again, and she soon became the happiest pixie anyone had ever known.

Richard's Mum

Luke 15:1-3, 11b-32

> *The prodigal son's father could equally have been his mother, since mothers too are never quite what their offspring want!*
>
> *This is a story about Richard, who resents his mother's discipline and breaks out against it, just as the prodigal son broke out against his father.*

Richard was about seven or eight when he first realised his Mum wasn't perfect. It came as a great shock to Richard, for before that, he had assumed his Mum knew everything and was always right.

Richard's teacher had asked the class: "Who thinks their Mum will run in the Mums' race at Sports Day?" and a whole class of hands had shot up, including Richard's. But when he'd gone home and excitedly told his Mum about the race, she'd laughed and said: "No thanks! My running days are long gone!" And Richard had suddenly realised that at thirty-something his Mum was old and was probably wearing out already.

After that, Richard began to notice more and more little faults in his Mum. For instance, his friend John's mother always kept chocolate biscuits in the tin at home, and all John's friends were allowed to dive in whenever they felt like it. Sarah's Mum always held a party for Sarah's birthday each year and never moaned about the mess on the carpet afterward. Damien's Mum let Damien stay up really late and watch 15-rated films on television and even get out horror videos from time to time.

Richard's Mum didn't do any of those things. What's more, she made Richard clean his teeth every day, and tidy his room from time to time. And she always seemed to know exactly what he was watching on television, even when she was miles away in the kitchen.

The more Richard looked and compared his Mum with other people's Mums, the more he found to criticise in his mother. In the end, he decided to gently suggest some changes.

He wrote a list to his mother. It took a long time, because he couldn't write very fast, and his writing was so big it kept filling up all the paper. But he managed it at last. He was a polite boy, so he didn't say; "I want," he headed the list with: Things I would like, if possible.

Top of the list came more pocket money, because he only got 50p and most of his friends got a pound, and that didn't seem fair. Then there was staying up late to watch some good films on television, because all the PG films were so naf. Then came having friends round whenever he wanted, and having crisps and biscuits and Coke always available in the house. The list was quite long and ended with things like: his mother wearing smarter clothes, like Samantha's mother. And getting thinner, like Max's mother. And his mother not meeting him right outside the school gate every evening, but waiting down the road a little way, because that would be really cool.

When Richard gave the list to his mother, she didn't say much, but her face looked a bit kind of sad, especially when she got to the end of the list. It didn't seem to make much difference in Richard's life. Nothing changed. His pocket money didn't increase, and he still went to bed every night at the same time, and his mother still waited for him at the school gate.

Richard got more fed up. After all, he'd asked politely, the least he could have expected was a reply.

One day, he asked his mother whether he could go on his bike with his friends, over to the old disused railway station. She said: "No. It's too dangerous. I don't want you going there." Richard was so disappointed he stuck out his lower lip in rebellion and went anyway. After all, his friends were all allowed to go, so why shouldn't he? He decided never to ask his mother again, because the answer was always the same and it wasn't worth the effort. From now on, he'd do what he wanted, and never mind the consequences.

They had a great morning at the old station, playing on the tracks, climbing on the roof of the old building, running in and out through dilapidated doors, and playing hide-and-seek. There were loads of brilliant places to hide. Richard squeezed behind an old cupboard without a door in the waiting room and laughed to himself as he heard his friends clambering about on the roof and running round looking for him.

Then suddenly there was a terrible sound like a huge explosion, and the whole building shook, and there was a crashing all round Richard, who found himself choking with dust. Huge pieces of timber smashed down, and Richard thought it was probably an earthquake, for the whole building seemed to be collapsing. Then he felt a searing pain in his leg and that was the last he remembered.

When he woke, he was in a strange room with lots of figures in white coats moving silently around. Richard was terrified. He wondered whether he'd died and was in heaven. He longed for his mother with an enormous yearning. He began to cry quietly, and sobbed: "Mum! Oh Mum, where are you? Please come, please come."

A white-coated figure came and peered at him and mumbled something about hospital and then went away again. Richard couldn't stop crying. He was so frightened, and his leg hurt so much, and he felt kind of weird, sort of spaced out, and not really knowing what was happening.

Then out of the corner of his eye he noticed the door quietly open, and a figure slipped in. In an instant Richard's Mum was beside him, cuddling him in her arms and stroking his forehead in that way she always did. She didn't say anything, just smiled. But Richard felt an enormous wave of love wash over him. His tears dried and he relaxed and fell asleep again.

He kept waking for a few moments, then dropping off to sleep again. Every time he woke, his Mum was there, and he knew everything was all right.

It took a long time for Richard to get better and for his leg to mend, but his Mum was always around somewhere. When he was nearly better, she used to go away for short periods, but he always knew she'd come back.

And he always knew he'd never swap his Mum for anyone else in the whole world.

Luke's Grandpa

John 12:1-8

*When Mary used a jar of very expensive ointment to anoint Jesus'
feet, other people condemned her because they thought her action
was inappropriate and wasteful. But Jesus received her gift with
warmth and praised her.*

*This is a story about Luke, who had a close relationship with
his grandfather. One day Luke decided to show his grandpa how
much he loved him, so he gave him a gift other people thought
wasteful and inappropriate.*

Luke was happy. He was doing something he loved best, walking in
the woods with his grandpa. Grandpa was the most interesting person
Luke had ever met. When they were indoors, he'd often play the piano
for Luke, and he could play any tune Luke could name, without ever
looking at any music.

But it was even better out of doors. Grandpa knew the name of
every flower and every tree. He knew where to spot bird's nests, and
how to track foxes and badgers. He never minded poking about in pools
and water and filling jam jars with newts and tiddlers and frogs' spawn.
And he always had time. Luke would ask endless questions. Sometimes
they poured out of his mouth like a kind of torrent, and he couldn't
stop them. But Grandpa always listened carefully and always answered
thoughtfully.

But today, Luke was quiet. He was quiet because he was so happy
he thought he might burst. He was quiet because he was thinking. He
wanted to give something back to Grandpa. Something really special,
something that would somehow show Grandpa how much Luke loved
him, without having to say any words. Grandpa glanced at Luke quizzi-
cally from time to time but didn't disturb him or interrupt his thought.

Luke was busy over the next few weeks. He'd spotted the perfect gift
for Grandpa, and he set about raising the money to buy it. He did some

odd jobs like cleaning the car, and he saved his pocket money. He saved most of his dinner money too, and swore his sister to silence when she threatened to tell on him. The rest of the family kept asking him what he was doing, but he refused to let on. He managed to withdraw all his money from the savings bank without his mother knowing, by taking out small amounts each day.

At last he had enough money, and he bought his gift. Grandpa was coming for the weekend, so Luke was ready. When Grandpa sat down at the piano after lunch on Sunday, Luke quietly brought out his parcel and undid it. He stood his gift on top of the piano.

Everyone stared in complete silence. Then Luke's sister pointed to the gift and started to laugh loudly. Luke's dad said: "What on earth is that thing?" And Luke's mum said very crossly: "It's not Grandpa's birthday, you know. What do you think you're doing, spending money on tacky rubbish like that? It must have cost you a small fortune."

Grandpa didn't say anything. He looked at the gift thoughtfully and began to play. And as he played, the garish plastic figure started to writhe and dance, and its eyes began to flash on and off. The faster Grandpa played, the faster the figure moved, and when Grandpa slowed down, the figure slowed down too.

"What a waste of money!" sneered Luke's sister. "Mum, do you know how much they cost? I saw them in the shop. Luke must have spent all the money he has on that!"

"Is this true, Luke?" asked his mother. "We've been saving that money for you, to give you a good future. Don't you realise your father and I have to go without, to buy you nice things? Why did you spend so much? Why didn't you ask first? Anyway, there are lots of much better things you could've bought than that. You could've bought something useful, like sheet music or a CD or a gardening book. Grandpa would have liked that, wouldn't you, Grandpa?"

Grandpa looked at Luke and there were tears in his eyes. But he blinked very quickly, then he winked. Then he said: "Yes, music or a book or a CD would've been very useful." He picked up the plastic figure and cradled it in his hands. "But this is the best present I've ever had. When you get to my age, nobody gives you anything just for fun, any more. I've had my fill of useful presents in my life, but I've never had anything that is such fun. A dancing figure! And I'm not sure anybody has ever given me a surprise gift before, for no other reason than to say — I love you." He turned to Luke. "Thank you Luke," he said gravely. "I love you too, more than I can say."

Luke grinned, a huge, wide grin. He winked back at Grandpa and said: "Fancy a walk in the woods?" And Grandpa smiled back and went to fetch his coat.

The Search for Kingship

Luke 19:28-40

Jesus was an unusual king, with none of the pomp and ceremony generally associated with kingship.

This is a story about a royal prince, who was sent by his father the king to travel through time and space to discover how to be a king. He found many of the usual qualities associated with kingship, but it wasn't until he encountered Jesus riding into Jerusalem on a donkey, and experienced the subsequent events, that he finally discovered kingship.

"It is time," said the king. "Now you are eighteen years old, you need to discover what it means to be a king. I am growing old. Soon you will be crowned king of our land, but first, you must understand for yourself how to rule."

Prince Agadir groaned inwardly. "But father," he began, "I was born to be king! All my life people have been showing me what I must do. I've worked hard at my lessons and passed all my exams in the history of our land and of the world. I've studied politics and economics. I've sat in the Forum and listened to the cut and thrust of modern debate. I know how to behave in polite society, and I've watched you. What more do I need?"

The old king laughed. "My son, you must travel through time and space to find out about kingship for yourself. Look at kings in history and kings in the future. Sit in their courts to see how they rule. And most importantly, listen to their people."

"And how shall I know when I've found the best model of kingship?" demanded the prince. "I suppose some kings are better than others, but basically, a king's a king!"

"You'll know when you discover the right king," replied his father, "because you'll find yourself immediately transported back here to Eatonia. Until then, I'm afraid you just have to wander."

Prince Agadir packed reluctantly for the journey and climbed into the time machine. He thought an advanced civilisation might be the best place to start, so he set the parameters for the year 3052. Then he closed his eyes and waited. The time machine moved swiftly and silently through the centuries and woke the prince with a buzzer when the right time zone had been reached.

Prince Agadir stepped into a strange, silent world. The streets were empty, there were no large buildings, no people, and no means of transport, just small box-like structures that he took to be houses. The prince entered the largest box.

He found a being that looked only faintly human. It had a large head, with huge eyes and huge ears, but a very small nose and mouth. The being had two pairs of arms and hands sprouting from its head, but no body and no legs. The eyes were watching the four walls of the box, which were all computer-like screens, and the hands were all busy clicking various buttons on the screens. As Agadir watched, he saw robots moving from different stations in the box, bringing tiny amounts of food and drink to the creature and entertaining the creature through the screens.

Then one of the screens changed, and Agadir saw many more of the creatures. The creature in the house began to issue commands via the screen, and all the other creatures responded to the commands until the screen was a mass of thoughts. Prince Agadir thought how boring life would be if you didn't need to move or do anything for yourself. If you didn't even need much food because you had no body, and you communicated with others not in person, but only by thought. He was glad he wasn't transported back to Eatonia, for he didn't think he could stand being a king of the future.

Back in the time machine, he decided to try the other extreme and visit King Arthur. After all, King Arthur lived in the Age of Chivalry, so perhaps he was the model king that Agadir was seeking.

Prince Agadir stepped from the time machine into the royal castle on the Enchanted Isle of Avalon. Through the slits of windows in the great hall, he could see knights in shining armour riding chargers and jousting. He could see knights on foot, practising archery and fencing. It was very exciting. Inside the great hall was a round table where more knights were in conference. Prince Agadir quickly spotted Sir Lancelot and Queen Guinevere, and King Arthur who was wearing chain mail and a crown. This was more like it!

King Arthur was talking about a forthcoming battle, and the knights were discussing strategy. Each knight was allowed his say, but the final decision was King Arthur's. It was clear all the knights had great respect and love for their king and would die for him if necessary.

Prince Agadir thought King Arthur was the perfect model for kingship. He was brave and true. He cared about his people. He had a lavish court where his knights were expected to be gallant and chivalrous. King Arthur ruled firmly but with compassion. What more could a king do? Agadir felt sure he'd found the king he was looking for so he waited to be transported back to Eatonia. But nothing happened!

Reluctantly, Prince Agadir climbed back into the time machine. As he turned for a last look at the court of King Arthur, wishing he could have stayed there longer, Agadir caught his foot. He tripped and sprawled onto the console of the machine. Immediately the time machine silently took off. Agadir had no idea where they were going, and anyway, he'd hurt his foot, so he just sat back and closed his eyes.

When they stopped, Prince Agadir found himself in a hot country with dusty roads and palm trees. There were a few buildings but nothing that looked remotely like a palace. It was a pretty poor place. As Agadir limped along the road, he noticed a small procession approaching. A man who looked like a peasant was riding on a donkey, and quite a lot of people were dancing all round him, waving branches from the trees. Some of them were shouting: "Blessed is the king who comes in the name of the Lord."

Agadir laughed. A king? What did they know about kings? Where was the horse, the shining armour, or the crown? Agadir decided to join the procession and find out what was going on. Just then, the man on the donkey looked at him, and the man's eyes were so full of love that Agadir felt as though he was melting. Then he noticed the pain from his injured foot had disappeared, and before he knew what he was doing, he began to sing and dance with the rest of the crowd.

Prince Agadir discovered the man's name was Jesus. And Agadir found he wanted to stay with Jesus more than anything in the world.

He wanted to stay so much that he forgot about the time machine. He forgot about becoming a king and he forgot about his home at Eatonia. He stayed with Jesus. He followed Jesus everywhere, listening to his words, watching him heal ill people, and noticing how everybody felt special whenever they were with Jesus.

Agadir discovered he was happier than he'd ever been in his whole life. He wanted to go on forever, just being with Jesus. But then, something terrible happened. Jesus was arrested and there was some sort of trial, and that same day, Jesus was executed. Agadir felt as though his world had come to an end. He'd never known such sadness. His life felt terribly empty, and he wondered what to do. Then he remembered Eatonia, and his quest for the perfect king, and he groaned, for he thought he might never find the king for whom he was searching.

But to his surprise, he suddenly found himself back in his father's palace in Eatonia. "You've done well," said his father. "I didn't expect you to find the king so quickly." Agadir frowned. "But I haven't found a king! I went to the future and that was hopeless. I went to the past but somehow it wasn't quite right. Then I ended up by accident with someone called Jesus, but he wasn't a king."

"Wasn't he?" said Agadir's father.

Agadir frowned. "He can't have been. He didn't look like a king, he looked like an ordinary person. He didn't seem like a king. He didn't give any orders. He was gentle and kind and loving. He didn't even have a proper court. It was clear he had no wealth. And now he's dead. So he can't have been a king."

Agadir's father smiled. "Look behind you, Agadir."

The prince turned and gasped. There stood Jesus in shimmering light, so glorious that Agadir had to shield his eyes. "Jesus?" he stammered.

"Welcome, Prince Agadir," said Jesus, softly. "I died, but God raised me from death and I can never die again. I will be with you for as long as you live."

Agadir knelt before Jesus. At last he understood. The trappings of kingship weren't important at all. What mattered was what was inside a person. Anybody could be a king, if they were like Jesus. Agadir knew he was now ready to be king, for all he had to do was follow Jesus.

The Parable of Bamboo

John 20:1-18

Once upon a time in the heart of a certain kingdom, lay a beautiful garden. Of all the dwellers of the garden, the most beautiful and beloved to the master of the garden was a splendid and noble Bamboo. Year after year, Bamboo grew yet more beautiful and gracious. He was conscious of his master's love, yet he was modest and in all things gentle. Often when Wind came to revel in the garden, Bamboo would dance and sway merrily, tossing and leaping and bowing in joyous abandon. He delighted his master's heart.

One day the master spoke: "Bamboo, I would use you." Bamboo flung his head to the sky in utter delight. The day in which he would find his completion and destiny had come! His voice came low: "Master, I am ready, use me as you want."

"Bamboo," the master's voice was grave, "I would be obliged to take you and cut you down." A trembling of great horror shook Bamboo. "Cut…me…down? Me whom you, master, have made the most beautiful in all your garden? Cut me down? Ah, not that, not that. Use me for your joy, oh master, but don't cut me down."

"Beloved Bamboo," the master's voice grew graver still. "If I do not cut you down, I cannot use you."

Bamboo slowly bent his proud and glorious head. Then came a whisper. "Master, if you cannot use me unless you cut me down, then do your will and cut."

"Bamboo, beloved Bamboo, I would cut your leaves and branches from you also."

"Master, master, spare me. Cut me down and lay my beauty in the dust but would you take from me my leaves and branches also?"

"Bamboo alas! If I do not cut them away, I cannot use you."

Bamboo shivered in terrible expectancy, whispering low. "Master, cut away."

"Bamboo, Bamboo. I would divide you in two and cut out your heart, for if I do not cut so, I cannot use you."

"Master, master, then cut and divide."

So the master of the garden took Bamboo and cut him down and hacked off his branches and stripped his leaves and divided him in two and cut out his heart and lifting him gently, carried him to where there was a spring of fresh, sparkling water in the midst of the master's dry fields. Then putting down one end of broken Bamboo into the spring and the other end into the water channel in the field, the master laid down gently his beloved Bamboo. The clear sparkling water raced joyously down the channel of Bamboo's torn body into the waiting fields. Then the rice was planted and the days went by. The shoots grew. The harvest came. In that day was Bamboo, once so glorious in his stately beauty, yet more glorious in his brokenness and humility. For in his beauty he was life abundant, but in his brokenness he became a channel of abundant life to his master's world.

(an ancient Easter story)

Thomas and the Cave

John 20:19-31

> *In this story, Thomas doubts the witness of his friends and is anxious about any change in the status quo. But once he sees for himself, he is convinced, and a whole new life full of promise, opens out before him.*

Thomas had never seen his friends so excited. Peter's eyes were shining, and he could hardly contain his impatience. John was always quieter than Peter, but even he seemed full of barely suppressed eagerness. They were both tugging at Thomas, while at the same time dancing round him.

Thomas reluctantly agreed to go to the cave with them, although he continued to think they were mad. "If there was nothing there last week, how can it have changed now?" he kept asking.

The other two dismissed his reservations with some impatience. "Come and see! When you've seen it for yourself, you'll know!"

The three of them had been visiting the cave for years. They'd kept it secret, and it had become a sort of gang headquarters for them, as with the help of torches, they'd explored every inch of it. It was a small cave fairly high up on the cliff face and very dark. The friends kept blankets and some food there. They were pretty sure no one else knew of the cave, for the entrance was just a narrow fissure in the cliff face, very difficult to spot from the sea, and only accessible to the boys at low tide.

Yesterday, Thomas had gone into the city with his parents, so Peter and John had visited the cave without him. When Thomas returned from the city, they were waiting on his doorstep, bursting with excitement. They told Thomas they'd found a tunnel at the rear of the cave, leading to another much larger cave, full of stalagmites and stalactites. Thomas had laughed. He knew it was impossible, for he'd meticulously examined all the walls of the cave himself, and there'd been no gap anywhere.

Thomas had always loved going to the cave. It had become a very special place for him, where he could be alone with his thoughts even when the others were around. But now, he found himself strangely reluctant. His feet dragged as Peter and John tried to chivvy him along. Part of him had caught their mood of excitement, and longed for their tale to be true, but most of him was certain they were wrong, even though he didn't want them to be wrong. He wanted to find a tunnel and another cave to explore, and try as he would, pictures of treasure kept filling his mind. But he was so very afraid he'd be sadly disappointed, and there'd be nothing worthwhile. And if that happened, somehow it might be the end of all his dreams.

Thomas wanted to keep the cave special. Peter and John kept telling him it was even more special now, in a different sort of way, but he wasn't convinced. If he went expecting something terrific from the cave, but it didn't happen, Thomas knew the cave would be forever spoiled for him. He'd never feel the same about it again. Somehow, he'd be plunged into the next stage of growing up, and he didn't feel quite ready for that.

When the three of them reached the cave after the usual long climb up the cliffs, Thomas felt kind of shivery and expectant. He could feel his heart hammering inside his chest as he followed the others into the cave. Thomas shone his torch onto the far wall as Peter and John felt carefully along it. Thomas couldn't see anything except rock, and the other two seemed to be having some difficulty finding whatever it was they were seeking.

Thomas' spirits began to sink even lower as he watched his friends. Then John cried out: "It's here! Here it is!"

Thomas immediately shone his torch in John's direction, but he could see nothing other than rock. He moved over to John and noticed his friend had his hands high up on the rock and was feeling all round a little outcrop of stone. Then Thomas gasped, for a narrow gap had appeared in the wall from nowhere, just wide enough for a boy to squeeze through.

The three boys slid silently through the gap and crawled along a low tunnel. It was scary and a bit suffocating and pitch black except for the torches, and for a moment, Thomas felt real fear. But all thoughts of fear vanished as the tunnel widened into a huge cave, faintly lit by a shaft of sunlight entering from high up in the roof.

The cave was astonishing. There was a little river running along the floor and crazy rock formations at various points. Stalagmites grew up from the floor, some of them meeting stalactites, which were growing downward from the roof. The sunlight was glistening on different minerals in the rocks, which sparkled and shone like jewels. The three boys stood gazing, awe-struck.

Thomas with his torch inched slowly around the perimeter of the walls and to his amazement, discovered the walls were covered in what looked like ancient paintings of birds and animals. Thomas was captivated. He thought he'd never seen anything so exciting and so beautiful, with a strange far away sort of beauty. He felt a deep urge to learn more about the people who had painted the cave, who they were, where they came from, how long ago they'd lived, who they'd worshipped.

He also knew instinctively this was an important find and couldn't be kept secret. The three boys would have to reveal their cave to the authorities, which would mean they'd never be able to use it again just for themselves. For just a fleeting moment Thomas was sad about that. He'd dreaded losing the cave in some way, but now that it was happening, he felt all right about it.

He knew he'd taken a big step out of childhood, but strangely, it felt good. Suddenly, Thomas was ready — because he knew now what he was going to do with his life. He'd never seen anything as marvellous as those cave paintings before, and he knew he was going to spend the rest of his life exploring paintings just like them. He was going to be an anthropologist and learn everything there was to learn about ancient peoples.

A little bit of Thomas died in that cave, the part that belonged with childhood memories. But as a whole new world opened up before him, he was able to lay those childhood memories to rest. He had a glimpse of a vast, new future, and he looked and saw that it was very good.

The Mystery of the Marshes

John 21:1-19

> *This story is about two children lost on the marshes in the mist. In the mist, things look different. Everything appears to be grotesque and forbidding. When the children spot a strange and frightening figure, they have to decide whether or not to trust their instincts and risk going to the figure and possible salvation.*

Cley marshes (pronounced Cly), are rich in wild life, especially sea birds. Twice a day, when the tide comes in, the marshes tend to flood, despite the high sea defence wall that has been built along the shore. But this constant watering nourishes the sea flora and fauna, which inhabit the marshes.

From the coast road, which runs along the side of the marsh, there's not all that much to see. Just a vast flat expanse of sea heather and sea lavender, interrupted by little rivulets and pools, and occasionally by clumps of fairly solid, grassy earth. But once on the marsh itself, if you tread carefully from clump to clump, a new world opens up. A world of tiny creatures, unexpected flowers, and a host of sea birds, some of them rarely seen outside Cley marshes.

Robin and Bethany had spotted "their" marsh heron. The heron wasn't particularly rare, but it was an elegant and beautiful bird Robin and Bethany liked to think of as their own. They'd watched the heron in flight, they'd watched it feeding, and they'd watched it waiting still as a stone statue for the exact moment to strike with its long, sharp beak. The children had a proprietary feeling toward the heron, and whenever they could, they stalked it over the marshes.

Having been born and brought up in the little cottage on the coast road, Robin and Bethany knew the marshes almost as well as they knew their own back garden. Indeed, they regarded the marshes *as* their back garden, for the marshes provided an endless and constantly changing playground for the children. The marshes were designated an area of outstanding natural beauty, and therefore qualified for a warden. Robin and Bethany's father was warden and had taught his children a deep love and respect for the marshes.

"Come on," cried Robin, and the two of them took off, silently following the heron. This time, almost as though it knew their plan, the heron playfully led them deep into the marshes. But the children knew how to distinguish firm ground from marshy deeps, and they followed with confident, sure feet.

That is, they followed with confident, sure feet until the mist came down. All the coastal areas of North Norfolk are prey to sea fret from time to time, and Cley is no exception. Usually the children were alert to any sudden change in temperature and skipped quickly home, but today they were deep in the marshes and concentrating on the heron rather than on the weather.

Bethany noticed it first. She felt a sudden chill through the thick fabric of her sweatshirt, and she looked up. She tugged at Robin's arm. "Look! It's the fret!"

"We'd better go back," said Robin, the elder of the two, and turned to lead the way. But the mist had descended thickly and silently and the two children were further into the marsh than they'd ever been before, and they were quickly disorientated. They could no longer see very far ahead, and the coast road had long since disappeared. They trod a few clumps but everything looked different in the mist, and it had such a deadening effect. The children could no longer hear the sounds of the marsh, which were swallowed whole by the fog. It was weird and scary, and already very cold.

"What'll we do?" asked Bethany, feeling smaller than she could ever remember feeling. The fog had that effect. In the marsh fog, you became nobody, because the fog was so huge and so overpowering and so numbing and so relentless.

Robin shivered. "Follow me," he ordered, "but be very careful to put your feet exactly where I put mine. I can't see the clumps any more, so I'll just have to feel for them. And hold my hand, we must keep together."

It was slow progress, feeling for every footstep. Gone was the light-hearted skipping, leaping confidently from tuft to tuft. Once Bethany felt her foot slip into icy water and she cried out, but Robin pulled her clear. The two children clung together, frightened and lonely.

In the end, Robin stopped. He had an uneasy feeling they'd been going in circles, although he had no means of checking since he couldn't make out any landmarks. Bethany sensed his fear and snuggled up against him. "It'll be all right," she whispered, although she had an uncomfortable feeling it might not be all right. Then she said, "What?" for she felt Robin stiffen.

He held her hand tightly. "Look, over there," he muttered anxiously.

Bethany looked and screamed. She couldn't help herself. A huge figure had suddenly loomed out of the mist. Bethany didn't know whether it was man or monster, for its massive shape was distorted by the fog and it kept appearing and disappearing. It had heard her scream and now a deep but muffled voice reached them over the mist. They could just make out the words. "Come to me. Over here."

The children looked at each other, terror in their eyes. Then Bethany whispered hopefully, "Do you think it might be Dad?" and all at once the figure appeared less threatening, and a great optimism burst upon the children.

They still hesitated, but not for long. "Come on," said Robin, "we have to risk it." And with some anxiety but with a scarcely admitted hope in their hearts, they began to make their way toward the waiting figure. When they got within a few feet, they recognised their father, and they ran into his warm and welcoming arms.

"Dad, is it really you?" whispered Bethany. But Robin declared, "I knew you'd come!"

And he was right.

St. Peter's Pool

John 10:22-30

> *This is a story about eight-year-old Sarah, who was unable to swim. Sarah longed to be able to swim but was frightened of the water. It became more difficult as she grew older, especially as her mum had been a county swimmer in her day. Eventually, on holiday in Malta, Sarah plucks up the courage to take a great leap of faith and never looks back.*

Sarah was on holiday in Malta with her parents. It was the first time she had ever been abroad, and she found she loved it. She loved the sun and the sand and the sea. She loved paddling in the shallows at the edge of the sandy beach, and occasionally, when she felt really secure in her armbands and the sea had no waves at all, she'd try a little swimming.

Sarah's mum was an excellent swimmer. As a schoolgirl, she'd swum for the county, and she'd tried to extend her love of swimming to Sarah. But for some reason neither of them could fathom, Sarah had always hated the water. Perhaps it had been too cold when she was just a baby, or perhaps she had slipped and experienced the terror of water relentlessly covering her face and her nose and her mouth and making her choke. Neither Sarah nor her Mum could remember anything like that, but they couldn't think of any other explanation for Sarah's instinctive fear. Sarah's dad wasn't unduly keen on any sport, but even he was a moderate swimmer and enjoyed a dip from time to time if the water was warm.

Neither of them had pressed Sarah. "It's okay, love," Sarah's Mum had said, comforting her daughter, "take your own time about it and don't worry! It really doesn't matter if you *never* swim! It's just that I think you'd learn to love it, once you got going. Once you can swim, a whole new world of excitement opens up for you. Water slides and Aqua Parks and snorkelling and water skiing and even deep sea diving if you wanted."

Sarah had nodded and felt even more miserable. It didn't really help to be told what she was missing. And the older she got, the harder it was to learn to swim, because it meant first admitting she *couldn't* swim, and at times she was sure she was the only eight-year-old in the whole world who was unable to swim.

But here in Malta, it was okay. Nobody knew whether she could swim or not, and nobody cared, so she could happily paddle on the edge of the water in her armbands and even take one foot off the bottom when nobody was looking.

The holiday wasn't only beach and swimming. Malta is quite a small island, but there was so much to see. Sarah discovered the island was steeped in history, and she particularly enjoyed exploring the caves and underground crypts where St. Paul and the early Christians had worshipped God.

One morning the family set off to visit St Peter's Pool, which they'd heard was a natural beauty spot. As they rounded the corner and came suddenly upon the pool, Sarah gasped. She thought she'd never seen anywhere so brilliant. It was a large, natural pool, surrounded by high rocks. It very deep and very clear. It was also deserted. For the first time in her life, Sarah longed to leap into the water and float lazily in the sunshine.

Sarah's mum dived in first. She seemed to go down and down and down, so that Sarah wondered whether she'd ever reappear. Sarah's dad sat on the rocks and kind of slithered in. He didn't like putting his face underwater, so he never jumped in. But as soon as he felt the water, his face took on a dreamy look, just as though he was in heaven.

Sarah's mum broke the surface of the water again, breathless and exhilarated. "Come on, Sarah," she called. "It's wonderful. You'd love it — and there's no one else here, no one watching. Do come in. I'll catch you."

Sarah looked longingly at the cool, clear water. "I haven't brought my armbands," she objected.

"Doesn't matter," replied her mother. "I'll catch you. I promise I won't let you go under."

Sarah hesitated. The sun was so hot, and here in the shelter of the rocks it was a natural suntrap with no breeze. It looked good in the

water, and her mum and dad seemed to be enjoying themselves. Part of
Sarah yearned to join them, but another part was unwilling to risk the
deep water. She couldn't swim, so perhaps she would drown.

Sarah dithered on the edge. She stuck her foot in the water, and it
felt delicious. She looked at her mum waiting patiently for her, but she
felt afraid. Swimming looked good, especially today, but was it really as
great as it looked? Perhaps she'd be better to remain on dry land where
at least she knew she was safe. Why take the risk?

As she turned sadly to go away, Sarah took one last look at the invit-
ing pool. Then suddenly she made up her mind, "Catch me, Mum," she
cried, "I'm coming!" And before she had a chance to change her mind,
she ran to the edge of the pool and launched herself into space.

For one terrifying moment she thought she was going under, then
she felt her mother's strong arms around her, and she was firmly held.
The water was marvellous, she'd never experienced anything quite like it.
It felt so different in the water. Sarah had never realised what deep water
felt like, she'd never been in deep water before. After a while, she got her
mother to hold her with just one hand, and she found she could swim.
Then her mother held her with just one finger, and again, Sarah swam.
Before very long, Sarah found herself swimming alone!

"I can do it! Look Dad," she shouted excitedly. "Look Mum, look
at me! I can swim! I'm really swimming, all by myself. Do you know, it's
so much easier to swim in deep water than it is in shallow water. And
it's much more fun. Mum, this is the best day of my life! I'm so glad I
dared to jump in."

From that day, Sarah never looked back. She never became a swimming champion like her mum, but swimming became her favourite activity as she gradually learned to trust both herself and the water. When
she went back to school after the summer holidays, she found she'd
become one of the best swimmers in the class.

Oh Bobby!

John 13:31-35

> *God loves us beyond anything we can imagine, and Jesus instructs us to love each other unconditionally, just as he loves us.*
>
> *This is a story that begins to explore the concept of love. The story is about Bobby, who overhears his parents talking about him, and misunderstands what they say. He begins to realise the extent of their love for him when they stand by him even though he's done something really bad.*

From a very young age, Bobby Hall knew he was a problem. He couldn't help getting into trouble, and his parents would sigh and say, "Oh Bobby!"

When he spilled treacle over the kitchen floor, or forgot to turn off the tap in the bathroom, or left the jigsaw all over the floor so that the dog chewed it up, his mother would shake her head and sigh, "Oh Bobby!" Lucy, his older sister copied their mother and sighed, "Oh Bobby!" And as soon as Polly, their younger sister could speak, she too began to shake her head and sigh, "Oh Bobby!"

Bobby generally pouted and stamped his foot and ran out of the room. Or sometimes he would scream or roar for added effect. When he felt really fed up, he'd scream and roar and stamp and kick somewhere near his sisters, because that usually made them cry and made Bobby feel a lot better.

He knew he was really bad, when he overheard his parents talking about "middle child syndrome." Bobby knew he was the middle child in the family, and he knew from Sunday school that sin was bad, even though he didn't really know what "drome" meant. He thought perhaps it was especially bad sin, because he knew an aerodrome was a very big place for airplanes, so perhaps "sin-drome" was very big sin.

For a while, Bobby Hall felt quite miserable knowing he was such an awful person. But then he decided if he was that bad, he'd better start acting as bad as he could be. And then he began to enjoy it, especially at school. He discovered that when he put little spots of glue on the teacher's chair, the other children loved it. They treated him with awe, and he became quite a hero in school. His teacher was often heard to sigh, "Oh Bobby!" but the children sang, "Oh Bobby!" in quite a different tone of voice.

Bobby's early success with the glue started all sorts of ideas in his mind. He became quite deft with glue, quietly sticking down the corners of envelopes so that they became almost impossible to open, and adding just a touch of glue to the class register, so that two pages were constantly sticking together.

But his best idea came when he stumbled across a large pot of superglue in his dad's garage. Bobby's mind sparkled, his eyes gleamed. He slipped the glue quietly into his school bag and set off for school. While the other children were playing in the school playground before the bell went, Bobby slid into his classroom as silently as a ghost. He set to work very quickly, then glided out into the playground in time to join in with a game of football with his friends.

When the bell went, the children lined up in the playground and marched into school. Bobby's class sat down. "Open your desks," said the teacher, "and find a reading book while I take the register."

She pulled at the lid of her own desk, but it remained firmly shut. The children pulled and heaved but not a single desk would open. The teacher was furious. "Who's responsible for this?" she asked. "Bobby Hall, stand up. Is this something to do with you?"

"Me, Miss?" said Bobby, looking hurt and innocent. "I've been playing football. Haven't I?" he appealed to his friends.

"Yes, Miss," they chorused, "Bobby's been with us."

The teacher went off to find the Headmaster, who came back looking very stern. He tried to open a couple of desks, but in vain. He gave the children a long lecture about the seriousness of damaging school property, and that they might have to call in the police, if no one owned up. Bobby didn't hear any of the lecture. He was busy dreaming up his next scheme.

After an unpleasant week or two, while all the teachers walked around with grim faces looking suspiciously at all their pupils, the fu-

rore died down and seemed to be forgotten. Nobody had actually accused Bobby, although several had given him accusing looks, and Bobby
felt rather pleased with himself. That is, until his father wandered into
the garage one day and discovered his large pot of superglue was nearly
empty.

Bobby was called before his parents. "Bobby, did you glue those
desk lids down?" asked his father.

Bobby looked miserably at the floor. "Yes," he muttered.

"Why? What on earth possessed you to do such a thing? Don't you
know you should respect other people's property? The desks belong to
the school. Not only have you stolen a day's education from every child
in your class, but you've caused the school a great deal of expense. What
do you have to say about that?"

"I'm sorry," mumbled Bobby.

His father sighed. "Oh Bobby! I wish we could help you. It feels like
you shut us out of your life, then try to be popular with the other kids by
doing terrible things. One day, you'll really hurt someone. I don't want
that to happen to you."

Bobby frowned. Then he shouted, "You don't love me! You love
Lucy and Polly, but no one loves me!"

His parents stared at him, their mouths open. Then his mother
hugged him and said, "We love you very much Bobby, but you're always
too busy trying to be bad to notice."

"You must go to the Headmaster tomorrow and apologise," said
Bobby's father. And no matter how Bobby protested and cried and
screamed and stamped, his father was adamant.

In the morning, Bobby's heart sank as he watched his parents put
on their coats. They were evidently going to deliver him to the school
gates, so escape was impossible. But when they reached the school, to
his surprise they stayed with him. They each held his hand and walked
with him to the Headmaster's office. Once inside, Bobby's dad kept a
protective arm around his son's shoulders, and Bobby's mum continued
to hold his hand.

To Bobby's amazement, his dad spoke up for him. He told the
Headmaster what Bobby had done, but said Bobby was good deep

down inside, there was no real badness in him. Bobby couldn't believe his ears. His dad thought he was good?

"What about middle child sin-drome?" he blurted out. "How can you love me when I have all that sin inside me? Even though I'm sorry, nothing can change that. I'm just wicked because of my sin-drome."

All the grown-ups began to laugh, and Bobby's dad explained that syndrome meant a set of symptoms, that middle children sometimes feel unloved and left out, even though they're not.

"I think from now on," he said, "we shall have to talk about middle child love-drome, because we love you so much."

And Bobby suddenly realised that was true. His parents loved him so much that they didn't excuse what he'd done wrong, but they were alongside him all the way when he went to confess and face his punishment. They'd even given up a day's work each to go with him to the Headmaster.

The Headmaster suggested that as Bobby was so fond of glue, he should spend every spare moment for the next month making a match-stick model of the Houses of Parliament for the Infant's Class.

Bobby's dad helped him make the model and Bobby discovered he loved making it. It took such a long time that Bobby quite forgot to be bad. And when it was finished he felt so proud of it, and so anxious to start another model, that he knew his "sin-drome" days were over forever.

Everybody who looked at the model sighed, "Oh Bobby!" but this time, Bobby didn't mind at all.

Jenny and the Missing Calculator

John 5:1-9

> *The story in John 5:1-9 tells only half the truth. When the whole
> story is read (ending at v. 17), a different picture of the character
> of the healed man emerges. Today's story is about a half-truth that
> pointed away from the real truth and caused all sorts of distress to
> Jenny and a number of other people.*

Jenny was having fun. Her friend Martha had brought a graphical calculator into school. Martha had borrowed the calculator from her older
brother, who used it for his advanced maths. He'd been off school for a
week, so Martha had figured he wouldn't need his calculator for a while.
She and Jenny had soon discovered a great bowling game hidden in the
depths of the calculator, and Jenny, to her excitement, had just reached
level three.

As the bell sounded for the next lesson, Martha asked for her calculator back. "Hang on a minute," said Jenny. "I just want to finish
this game. I'll give it back in a minute." So Martha went on her way.
She forgot all about the calculator until that evening, when her brother
roared at her.

"Oh shut up!" said Martha. "It's no big deal. I'll get it back tomorrow at school." But it was an uncomfortable evening. Martha's parents
kept nagging her about borrowing the calculator without permission,
and her brother was bad tempered and grouchy.

As soon as she reached school the next day, Martha sought out Jenny. "Can I have the calculator back, please?"

Jenny stared at her. "I gave it back yesterday."

"What? You didn't! When I asked you for it, you said you wanted
to finish that game."

"But I came straight afterward and found you in the loos. You were
talking to Emily and trying out her make-up. I said, 'Here's your calculator, Martha,' and put it down by your bag. Don't you remember?"

"I never saw it. I never saw you, come to that," frowned Martha. "Are you sure? Anyway, where is it now? I need it for my brother."

The two girls went to the toilets, but there was no calculator there. "Someone must have found it and handed it in," suggested Jenny. "I'll try Lost Property."

There was no calculator in Lost Property. Martha was desperately worried. She knew the calculator was very expensive. "It's all your fault!" she shouted at her friend. "You didn't give it back to me."

"I did," protested Jenny. Then she added, "Look, if we can't find it, I'll give you something toward the cost of a new one." But Martha refused to be consoled. All sorts of nasty suspicions were beginning to fill her mind. She had no recollection at all of having seen Jenny in the cloakroom, although it was true she had been in there with Emily trying on make-up. But Jenny couldn't have come in without her noticing! Anyway, she'd have noticed the calculator when she went to pick up her bag. Jenny must be lying. And why would she lie? Jenny must have stolen the calculator!

The more she thought about it, the more Martha became convinced Jenny had stolen the calculator. There was no other explanation. She told her parents of her suspicions that evening, and her father rang Jenny's home, without actually accusing Jenny of theft, but implying their suspicions. Jenny's mother immediately offered to pay half toward a replacement, which reinforced Martha's family's view. "Why would she offer to pay half?" asked Martha's mother. And added, "Because she'll be getting a graphical calculator for half price, that's why!" and the family refused to accept the offer. It was still uncomfortable for Martha at home, but at least the anger of her family was now directed rather more toward Jenny than toward her.

"We'll make her pay!" fumed Martha's mother. "How dare she think she can get away with nicking an expensive item like that? Ring again tomorrow night," she instructed her husband.

Martha found she was unable to speak civilly to Jenny at school. All Martha's friends formed a protective group around her and shouted at Jenny that she'd have to pay up or else.

Jenny looked deeply unhappy. "Have you seen the Head?" she asked Martha. Martha flushed. "Of course I have," she shouted angrily. "What do you think I am? Stupid?"

Jenny bit her lip and looked worried. "I'll go and ask again in Lost Property," she offered.

Things went from bad to worse. Jenny's mother continued to offer to pay half the cost of a new calculator; Martha's family continued to refuse, hinting all the time at theft by Jenny.

In the end, Jenny's mother approached the school. She went to the Head and explained Jenny's version of the whole story.

The Head was very understanding. "I think your offer is very reasonable," he said. "I'll talk to Martha about it and I'll make some inquiries. Someone may have handed it in somewhere."

At lunchtime that day, both Jenny and Martha were called into his office. "Good news," he smiled. "Martha, I found your calculator under a pile of my books. It must have been there all week. What a pity neither of you came to me in the beginning."

Jenny gasped and looked at Martha, who went very red and looked at the carpet.

When they were out of the office, Jenny tackled her. "You told me you'd been to the Head," she accused Martha.

Martha retorted, "No I didn't! You asked if I'd seen him, and I said yes I had. That's all. I didn't tell any lies."

"But it was only half true," said Jenny, "and look at all the trouble it's caused between us! If I'd have known the truth, I would have gone myself. I'm not afraid of visiting the Headmaster's office. As it is, I don't suppose I shall ever be able to come to your house again. It's the end of our friendship. And your brother could have had his precious calculator back last week if only you'd been truthful! How can you live with yourself?"

Martha pouted and shouted rudely after her. She handed over the calculator when she got home, but somehow, she didn't feel any relief. Although she wouldn't admit it to herself, deep down inside she was sad to have lost Jenny, for she had a feeling Jenny was a good friend to have.

"That girl must have slipped the calculator into the Head's office when she got frightened she'd be found out as a thief," declared Martha's mother.

But Martha just sighed and felt very miserable.

The Bully-Busters

John 17:20-26

> *This is a story about three boys who put their lives at risk by trying to live according to the Christian principles of love and honesty. They get hurt in the process but discover that the love they experience binds them in a very special kind of unity.*

"I think," proclaimed Peter, lying on his back and gazing up at the trees, "we should become bully-busters."

"What?" said Jimmy, lazily. Karl simply rolled over, chewing at the blade of grass in his mouth.

"No, c'mon," said Peter. "Like ghost busters. We could identify all the bullies in school, then go bust them."

Karl laughed. "You mean you could! Jimmy and me'd just pick up the pieces afterward! Anyway, how you think you're gonna bust a gang like the Robots?"

Peter shrugged. "You know what they told us at Sunday school. Good always triumphs over evil in the end. We'll obliterate them with goodness."

"Now I know you're nuts," declared Jimmy. "You don't believe all that stuff, do you? We'd be dogmeat in seconds. Anyway, look what happened to Jesus! He got killed — and that's what'd happen to us! No thanks!"

"Come on, guys," urged Peter. "You don't like those bullies, do you? We don't have to do much. Just be honest with them and tell them what we really think and not run away from them."

His two friends looked at each other. "He's serious!" said Jimmy. "They'll kill us, you know they will. At least we survive at the moment."

"But what sort of a life do we have? They steal our pocket money and push us around and are always getting us into trouble. I'm fed up with it. We've tried hitting back, but that didn't work — they just laughed. We've tried telling, but they just got worse. What have we got to lose? Anyway, we'll have God on our side."

Karl and Jimmy were worried; they weren't at all sure how much protection God would actually offer. But they knew Peter in moods like this. He was the impulsive one, always acting first and thinking afterward, when it was too late. They could tell he was determined to go ahead with his hare-brained plan, which was doomed from the start, so either they went with him and tried to protect him from himself as best they could, or they let him go alone and probably get killed.

They talked on a bit, trying to dissuade their friend, but it was hopeless from the start.

"All right," they eventually agreed miserably. "We'll come. All for one and one for all. But if this doesn't work, you've had it! We'll kill you ourselves if the Robots don't!"

The three friends organised a few basic ground rules. When they met the gang, they'd always speak and answer absolutely honestly, even if this meant annoying the Robots, but wouldn't deliberately antagonise them. They would stand their ground, whatever happened. They would defend themselves, but not otherwise fight, and they wouldn't throw punches even in self-defence. They would no longer go out of their way to avoid the Robots but would choose routes whether the Robots were likely to be there or not.

It wasn't long before the plans were put to the test, for the three friends found the Robots blocking their way as they turned the corner past their school. Three hearts began to hammer against three sets of ribs, three pairs of knees began to tremble and three mouths suddenly felt very dry.

"So, what have we here?" jeered James Kinley, the leader of the gang. "You kids got any money?"

"Yes," said Peter, "I've got my pocket money."

James looked surprised at such a ready response. "Hand it over, then," he ordered. "You know the rules."

"No," said Peter.

"What? You stupid or something? You know what'll happen to you!"

"Yes, you'll beat me up and steal my money."

"Well hand it over then!"

"No."

As the four bigger boys took a menacing step forward, Karl and Jimmy closed in toward their friend. Jimmy felt almost resigned. This was madness. It would probably put them all in the hospital. But they'd made a pact and now they had to see it through. Bully-busters, indeed! The only ones who'd be busted were themselves, not the bullies.

Suddenly he became aware of one of the Robots peering at him. "You afraid?" sneered Tom Butcher.

Jimmy nodded. He knew the worst possible mistake was to admit fear in front of a bully, but he'd promised to be truthful. He felt like jelly as he waited for the first punch and clenched his fists ready to bring them up in front of his face. Perhaps he'd be able to stave off the first few blows.

But Tom was frowning. "Why don't you just give us the money then? Or leg it down the road or something? What are you doing just standing there?"

Jimmy thought carefully. He wanted to tell the absolute truth. "I don't want to be here," he said. "I am afraid of you all, and I'd rather be a million miles away. But I don't think you should steal our money. And Peter is my friend, so I'm not leaving him here alone."

Chris Weston was dancing about with glee. "Let's beat 'em up!" he cried. "That way we get their money and show 'em! Don't waste time talking to 'em, stupid little gits!"

But the others were looking uncertain and puzzled. This was a new response, one they hadn't met before. They turned to James for guidance.

A grin split James' face. Suddenly he grabbed Karl and dragged him away from the other two. "Now I'm going to bash him and you two sissies are just going to stand there and watch me," he cried and lifted his fist.

But Peter and Jimmy ran to their friend's side. "You'll have to bash us all," warned Peter.

"That can be arranged!" and he started to pound Karl, who curled away from him, trying to ward off the blows. "What's the matter, don't you like me?" taunted James.

Karl found enough breath to say, "No, I don't like anything about you. I feel sorry for you 'cos I know your dad walked out, and you have to live with your mum's boyfriends, but I don't like you. I think you bully because no one likes you and bullying is the only way you get what passes for respect."

There was a brief pause in the rain of blows as James registered Karl's remarks, then James went beserk, hitting and punching and kicking, with arms and legs flailing. His three gang mates piled in on top, and Peter, Jimmy, and Karl were soon bruised and bleeding. But all three refused to hit back.

They were all badly injured that day. Peter was taken to the hospital, unconscious. Karl and Jimmy were patched up in Casualty, but Jimmy had a broken arm, and Karl had fractured ribs, and both had badly swollen and bruised faces.

Jimmy felt deeply depressed, it hurt so much, and he was worried about Peter. Karl was silent, shocked by the ferocity of the attack. He wondered whether he'd ever find the courage to venture out of doors again. He found he hated James and his Robots, and the strength of his hatred scared him.

Peter came out of the hospital in a couple of days, but it was a week before any of their injuries had healed sufficiently to allow them to return to school. Peter's dad took all three of them in his car. He hadn't said much about the fight but the grimness of his look had been enough.

The three friends were called into the Headmaster's office. To their surprise, they saw the Robots there too but all looking very anxious and miserable. "I think these boys have something to say to you three," said the Head.

Each of the Robots in turn came and stood before Peter, Jimmy, and Karl. Each one looked crestfallen and ashamed and sad and each one in turn said, "I'm sorry. I didn't mean to hurt you so much."

Karl found his hatred evaporating. Why, the Robots weren't to be feared after all! All they could do was beat people up and when that didn't work, the Robots had nothing left. They were just sad and lonely. They had nothing.

The three friends looked at each other. They each had a tremendous feeling of love for each other. They had shared something very important, and they'd seen it through — despite the consequences. Somehow, there was a very special bond between them now, one which no one could break.

"We were bully-busters after all," said Jimmy, wonderingly. "And I think you may be right, Peter. In a funny sort of way, good does conquer evil, even though it hurts in the process! Let's go on busting bullies, it feels good."

Peter grinned. "But perhaps not every week! Let's hope it's only necessary now and again!"

Baby Genie's New Home

John 14:8-17 (25-27)

> *Using the idea of a friendly genie, this story attempts to address the idea of God being "within" human beings through his Spirit and opens up the possibility of communication with that god within, who will help and support as necessary.*

BG was very frightened. He'd never been out alone before, and he discovered he didn't know what to do. Especially as LG, his companion in crime, had suddenly and mysteriously disappeared.

Genies, as everyone knows, are *never* allowed out of their homes. Baby Genie knew that perfectly well. But Little Genie, who was a thousand or so years older than BG, didn't care about the rules. He never listened when older and wiser genies said, "It's for your own good." So when a tiny crack appeared in LG's bottle, he vapourised himself through it. Then he hovered over BG's old lamp, calling and pestering BG through the spout until BG too slid out of his lamp in a tiny puff of smoke.

But now LG had disappeared. Part of BG's fear was that this was exactly what the older and wiser genies had warned would happen. "Genies are born to serve," they had said. "Genies may live outside as slaves ready to do their master's bidding, but after they have fulfilled three wishes, they *must* return to their homes. Otherwise they atomise into their constituent molecules and disseminate into the air." BG remembered yawning at that point. He hadn't really understood what all those long words meant, but now, in the centre of his being, he was sure they meant LG had disintegrated and become part of the air, never to be seen as a genie again.

BG shivered. He wondered if he was next. He tried to squeeze back through the spout of his lamp, but somehow or other it acted like a valve, and would only allow one-way traffic. Then he wondered whether he could find a master. Perhaps if he lived as a slave for a while, then he could return and live in comfort in his lamp for the next thousand or so years. The only problem was, he didn't know how to be a slave, for he was too young to have attended Genie School.

BG hovered for a while but none of the older and wiser genies appeared to roar at him, or to help him, so he decided to explore. Being a genie, he had no wings, but he discovered that if he closed his eyes and thought very hard, he could float around on the air like a cloud. If he squeezed hard at one end of himself, and opened out at the other, he found he could move quite easily.

It was fun at first. He dipped into the local funfair, which was brilliant — except that he could only watch. After a while he got bored watching other people enjoy themselves. An imp of mischief began to stir in his mind, and all at once he realised why genies have such a bad reputation as evil spirits. No wonder they either had to act as slaves or be kept shut up. Genies grow so bored watching but not taking part that their active brains soon seek to hatch ways in which they might disrupt the normal smooth flow of human life. And since they live for thousands of years, genies have plenty of opportunities to refine their mischief.

BG sighed. He wasn't yet old enough to be bad. He was only a baby, and he didn't want to be bad. But he did want to do something, and he had a nasty feeling he might be shrinking by the minute. If he didn't soon find some sort of new home, he might suffer the same awful fate as LG.

Just then, BG heard a strange sound. It was a rasping, coughing sound, as though someone was struggling to breathe. BG followed the sound. He swooshed gently round a dark corner, and there, huddled into the shadow was a small human being, coughing and gasping for breath. BG didn't stop to think. He saw an open mouth and air being sucked in, and instantly materializing within the air, was sucked into the human being.

It was a strange journey, although BG felt quite warm as he was sucked down hundreds of tubes like the branches of a tree that became gradually smaller and smaller. The final tube was so tiny it was nearly impossible for the air to get through. BG felt great shudders as the chest of the human being heaved and gasped, so he pushed the tube a little more open and slid into a vast open space full of air, quite easily. The shuddering stopped but the strange noises changed, and BG became aware his human being was sobbing.

BG felt a flood of compassion for his human being. All thoughts of mischief had fled. Now he had a new home, and he wanted to help in any way he could.

"What's the matter?" he whispered, deep inside the human being. To his surprise, there was an immediate answer, although he couldn't tell whether the words were spoken out loud or merely thought. "It's my asthma," came the reply. "I can't do anything, because every time I start to run or get excited, I have an asthma attack and I can't breathe."

This was terrible! BG knew from experience what it felt like to have to stand and watch. And he knew what mischief might result from that. He felt warm and close toward his human being.

"Don't worry," he promised. "I'll help you. Now I'm inside you, I can feel when you have an attack coming on. I'll keep the tubes open for you." He felt his human relax and noticed the tubes relax too and open a bit wider. He began to sing a soothing, gentle, genie lullaby, and as he felt his human grow happier and happier, so the tubes opened wider and wider. Soon his human was breathing normally and without difficulty.

BG curled up in his new home and went to sleep. He liked this human being, and it was much better than living in a cold, old lamp. And here he could be useful. Whenever the human wanted him, he'd be there to help, breathing as the human breathed, enjoying activity as the human enjoyed it. The more he could love his human being and help him to relax, the more they could do together.

BG smiled and snuggled up inside the human's chest. Suddenly his future was bright. For what better future could he have than someone to love and someone who might in time come to love him?

Mary Louise and Her Silent Companions

John 16:12-15

In this story, Mary Louise's dolls come to life on Midsummer's Eve, because Mary Louise herself gives them a kiss. She discovers something of herself in each of her dolls but only one doll acts in exactly the way Mary Louise would have wished. The allegories to God the Father, God the Son, and God the Holy Spirit are hopefully obvious!

Mary Louise was a little bit lonely. Not completely lonely, but just a little bit. With no brothers or sisters, Mary Louise spent quite a lot of time playing by herself, although not completely by herself, for Mary Louise had a number of silent companions, who were a great comfort to her.

Every night when she went to bed, Mary Louise would line up her silent companions on the foot of the bed and give them a big kiss. Then she'd sigh happily, climb into bed, and fall asleep very quickly, for she knew her silent companions were looking out for her.

Mary Louise loved all her silent companions, for they were all different. There was Lion Cub, who ought to have been fierce and growly, but was actually just soft and cuddly. Then there was Monkey, who had awfully long arms and a silly, lopsided grin. Both of these had been sewn by Mary Louise's grandma, several years ago.

Next to Monkey sat Ragbag, who was a dog of indeterminate origin. Mary Louise had bought Ragbag herself at the church jumble sale. She'd paid five pence for him, and her mother had tried very hard to persuade her to ditch Ragbag in the dustbin. "You don't know where he's been," Mary Louise's mother had said. "Ugh! He's so dirty! At least let me wash him." But Mary Louise had shouted and kicked and put on her parts (an old Norfolk expression), and Ragbag had stayed, unwashed.

The next in line to Ragbag was Blue Ted, who pretended to be a Teddy Bear but who had bright blue fur that was long and straggly and rather itchy if you got too close for too long. But Mary Louise loved him anyway.

All these silent companions were ranged on the lap of Panda, who was almost as big as Mary Louise herself. But the final silent companion was the one Mary Louise loved best. Chrysanthemum, the rag doll with bright pink plaits had been with Mary Louise from the beginning. They'd shared a cot when Mary Louise was a tiny baby and had been together ever since. When all the other companions were left behind, sitting in their neat row at the foot of the bed, Chrysanthemum went on holiday with Mary Louise, her pink head generally poking out of Mary Louise's backpack at a crazy angle. Chrysanthemum was dear and good and kind. She was always there when needed, and she never answered back.

Just occasionally, when Mary Louise felt a little more lonely than usual, she wished her silent companions weren't quite so silent but would talk to her and play with her and show they had minds of their own. But mostly, Mary Louise accepted them as they were, with all their in-built limitations.

One Midsummer's Eve, not realising there was magic in the air, Mary Louise arranged her silent companions in the time-honoured way, gave them a huge kiss, sighed over each one, climbed into bed, and instantly fell asleep. She slept long and deeply, but just after midnight was awakened by a strange shuffling sound. Sleepily she opened her eyes, then rubbed them twice and stared in astonishment. All her silent companions were moving, sliding off the bed one by one. Big Panda was helping each one down to the floor.

Mary Louise leaned over the side of the bed and watched. Monkey and Blue Ted were dancing. They made a strange pair, but Mary Louise had always known they were both mad. Lion Cub was practising his growling. He crouched very low, pretending to stalk Ragbag, and growled as deeply as he could in the back of his throat. It emerged as a funny kind of gruff mew.

But Mary Louise felt particularly concerned about Ragbag. He was cowering in terror and edging away from Lion Cub into a corner. Surely he knew Lion Cub was just a baby showing off? Mary Louise wondered whether to go to Ragbag's aid but discovered she couldn't move. Her mind was fresh and lively, but somehow or other her limbs and body felt as if they were weighted to the bed. She could only watch in dismay.

Her dismay increased when she saw Monkey and Blue Ted glance across at Ragbag and begin to laugh. He *did* look funny but couldn't they see how lovely and gentle he was underneath all that filthy, matted, woollen hair?

Lion Cub was gaining courage by the moment and beginning to look really threatening, almost as though he was grown up. Perhaps Panda would do something. Panda was so big, all the other silent companions must surely be afraid of him. But Panda was the only one to remain on the bed. Perhaps he was so big he thought he'd be unable to climb back on when the moment came.

Ragbag looked forlorn and frightened and lonely. Mary Louise's heart went out to him, for she knew just how he felt. She noticed a little something in each of her silent companions that reminded her of herself, although she didn't always like what she saw.

Monkey and Blue Ted, acting so silly and laughing at someone who was down on his luck. Lion Cub, growing bolder and bolder as Ragbag grew more and more timid. Panda, just sitting there, doing nothing to help. But then she noticed her favourite, Chrysanthemum. The pink-haired doll, who was only half the size of Ragbag, marched straight up to Lion Cub and began to scold him. Mary Louise listened in amazement as Chrysanthemum soundly berated Lion Cub, using exactly the words and tone of voice Mary Louise herself would have used. Lion Cub, looking very sheepish and ashamed and suddenly small again, backed off. But Chrysanthemum hadn't finished. She put her tiny arms as far around Ragbag as she could reach and hugged him.

"Why are you doing that?" asked Ragbag, forlornly. "Nobody else likes me, not even Mary Louise's mother. I'm dirty and smelly and I'm such a coward. All the others laugh at me."

"Stop feeling so sorry for yourself," ordered Chrysanthemum sternly. "Mary Louise loves you, and that's all that matters. Why, the way she loves you, you should be able to do anything! Stop your wailing and your tears, and be a — a — a dog!"

Ragbag looked astounded. "Mary Louise loves me? Really?"

"Of course she does," Chrysanthemum retorted. "She gave you her kiss, didn't she? That's why you're alive now. And it's about time you started to enjoy your life and make something of yourself. Come on, let's dance together."

A huge grin slowly split Ragbag's face. He gathered the pink doll into his arms and began to dance. The others crowded round and began to applaud. "Welcome, Ragbag," they cried. "We love you, too. But you're so much easier to love when you're happy. Now you're not afraid any longer, and not feeling sorry for yourself, we'll have a party."

And, do you know, that's exactly what they did, there on the floor of Mary Louise's bedroom. Mary Louise was so happy she fell right back to sleep again. When she woke up the next morning, all her silent companions were ranged at the foot of the bed exactly as she'd left them last evening. She might have thought she'd been dreaming, except that Ragbag still wore a big grin, and Lion Cub was nestled up against him, purring softly.

After that, Mary Louise was very careful how she behaved. For if her silent companions were alive through her spirit, she wanted them to enjoy the very best life they could.

The Great Chess Game

Luke 7:36—8:3

This is a story about Stephen, who cheats at chess in order to win. At the time he's not really aware of sin, but some years later he suddenly realises what he's done. He also realises forgiveness was there for him from the beginning, but he was only able to receive that forgiveness when he became aware of his sin. He discovers love and forgiveness are very close.

Stephen started playing chess when he was quite small. On his fifth birthday, his grandfather gave him a chess set and Stephen was hooked. He loved the feel of the smooth wooden pieces and he loved their shape, but most of all, he loved his grandpa.

Stephen's grandpa started to teach him how to play chess that very day. It was difficult and complicated, but Stephen concentrated and soon began to pick up the moves. After that, Stephen and his grandpa played chess together whenever they could. Stephen used to look forward all week to the weekend, when he knew he'd be spending an hour or more alone with Grandpa.

There was something about the old man. He was never in a hurry. It didn't matter how long Stephen dithered over his moves, Grandpa simply waited patiently until he was ready. And Stephen in his turn respected Grandpa's slowness, and his need to go to the bathroom at least once in every game. Grandpa was the only grown-up who allowed Stephen to be completely himself. He treated him not as a little kid but as seriously as he treated his own friends. It made Stephen feel very special.

There was only one problem for Stephen. He never won. No matter how hard he tried or how much he concentrated, Grandpa always beat him. Stephen learned about Fool's Mate the hard way. And he soon learned too about castling, Queen's Gambit, King's Side openings, and about "pinning" pieces and about the Fork, but he still lost. Somehow or other, Grandpa was always one step ahead. Occasionally, when he was really disappointed, Stephen would pout and frown like a small child, but Grandpa took it all in stride and it never put him off playing with Stephen. He'd usually nod wisely and say, "You're nearly there, Stephen. One day soon you're going to beat me, and then there'll be no stopping you. And when you do beat me, you'll know you did it all by yourself, because I'm always going to do my utmost to beat you!" And with that, Stephen had to be content.

It wasn't as if he never won. He could beat his older sister with his eyes shut, but she'd grown bored when Grandpa had tried to teach her, so she didn't really count. He could beat his dad most times, but his dad never had time to sit around playing games, so he wasn't much of a player. He could beat his mum, who was quite a good player because she'd been taught by Grandpa when she was a child, but Stephen always had the feeling his mum let him win from time to time because she felt sorry for him.

One day when Stephen was nine, he set out the board as usual, and sat down with Grandpa. Stephen was playing well. Grandpa was getting slower and slower with his moves, which meant he was having to think very hard indeed. Stephen felt a great excitement growing in him. Somehow he knew this was going to be The Day. With ever-increasing confidence he made his moves, until he moved a pawn to the wrong square, and regretted it immediately. But it looked as if Grandpa hadn't even noticed, for at that very moment he got up for one of his frequent trips to the bathroom. In a flash, Stephen had corrected his mistake and moved his pawn just one square. It made all the difference. When Grandpa returned the game continued, and for the first time ever, Stephen beat his grandpa.

He was elated. He'd never felt so thrilled or so proud of himself. Grandpa was delighted too and hugged and kissed him. "There," he said, "I knew you could do it. And I knew it wouldn't be long. Now you're really a player, and you'll go from strength to strength. You'll see."

Stephen did go from strength to strength. Chess continued to be the all-absorbing passion in his life, and he played whenever he could.

Then Grandpa became ill. He was taken to the hospital by ambulance, and Stephen felt as though his whole world was breaking apart. He went to the hospital to visit his grandpa, but the old man was too ill even to play chess. Stephen sat by his bedside holding his hand and not knowing what to say. Suddenly he blurted out, "Don't die, Grandpa. I couldn't bear it."

The old man managed a smile. "Don't grieve for me, Stephen," he said. "I shall be happy at that great chess game in the sky where winning or losing won't matter, just the enjoyment of the game."

Stephen stared at him with a little frown of remembrance. "Grandpa," he began, "there's something I have to say to you. Do you remember the first time I beat you? How thrilled we all were? Well, I cheated." And with that, Stephen began to sob, great heaving sobs that racked his whole body. Suddenly, after all this time, he was deeply ashamed of himself.

"My chess is all built on a lie," he wept. "I didn't beat you fairly. I cheated."

The old man patted his hand. "I know," he said.

"You know?"

"Of course. Did you really think I wouldn't notice you'd moved your pawn when I was out of the room?"

"But you didn't say anything! You hugged and kissed me as though I'd done it all by myself!"

Grandpa squeezed his hand. "I was sorry you felt you had to cheat, but I reckoned you'd have to sort that out yourself one day. You were wrong to cheat, but I couldn't stop loving you. It's you I love, not whether you win or lose, or even how you behave."

"So you forgave me right from that moment, even though I didn't really think I'd done anything much wrong?"

Grandpa nodded. "Of course. Forgiveness was always there, only you weren't able to receive it until now. But Stephen, you've made me so very happy. Now I shall die content that you've been able to acknowledge your wrongdoing and have therefore received the forgiveness that was waiting for you. Stephen, I love you so much. This is good-bye, but now you can play your chess for both of us. And one day, we'll meet again."

Grandpa died the next day, and Stephen was deeply sad for a long time. Somehow he grew up during that time and eventually he became a leading national chess player. More importantly, he became a much loved and respected man, someone of whom his grandfather would have been very proud. Because Stephen never forgot his grandfather and his grandfather's love and forgiveness and he never cheated again.

Praxis Finds Himself

Luke 8:26-39

Today's gospel reading is about Legion, the man who was possessed by so many demons he didn't know who he was. When Legion came into contact with Jesus, who was truly himself, he was healed. This is a story about Praxis the pixie, who tries to be something he isn't. He eventually realises he needs to become more himself, not less himself.

Praxis had a problem. It wasn't a problem shared by any of the other pixies, it was his alone and it was often very embarrassing.

From time to time, Praxis would change colour. Once, when he was sitting alone under a tree feeling rather sad, he noticed he'd turned bright blue. On another occasion, when one of his pixie friends proudly displayed a new miniature pixie computer in the shape of a daisy, Praxis turned a delicate shade of green. When feeling very jealous of his brother who had won a pixie race, Praxis had suddenly become a brilliant and shining yellow.

Most of the time, because he was a happy and healthy pixie, Praxis was the usual shade of pink, albeit a little brighter than most other pixies. He didn't mind that, but it was very uncomfortable when everybody knew exactly what he was feeling because of the colour of his pixie skin. Although sometimes, other pixies were sympathetic, and that was rather nice.

When Praxis was blue, they generally gathered round and did their best to cheer him up. And everybody clapped and shouted and felt much better when he gradually turned pink again. But sometimes, they kept their distance. When he was blazing red, no one would go near him, for his temper was famous and they knew he was angry. Even when the red died away and changed to a dull, dark grey, they were timid about approaching him, for they all knew how miserable he'd be.

Praxis thought it was very unfair. He never knew what other pixies were thinking or feeling, unless they told him. But the whole world could see how he was, just by looking at him. Sometimes Praxis felt uncomfortable with the others, as though perhaps they were hiding their real feelings. When that happened Praxis felt confused. He didn't know quite where he was with them, and he didn't know what to say or what to do. But he thought it was a very useful ability, and he wished he could hide himself too.

Praxis wondered whether he could pretend. Perhaps if he tried very hard to think and feel something different, he would be able to control his colour. The very next time he felt sad, he pretended to himself that he was happy. And to his delight, the blue colour began to fade, and was gradually replaced by pink. Praxis was so happy about his achievement, the pink grew brighter and brighter until he glowed in the dark.

When he was alone, Praxis started to work hard at controlling his colour. He learned to change pink to red by pretending to be angry. He learned to change green to pink, by pretending he didn't mind at all what exciting possessions other pixies had. He learned to change yellow to blue by pretending he wasn't really jealous, only sad.

It worked! Even though other pixies could see his colour, now they only saw the colours Praxis allowed them to see.

After a while, Praxis began to notice he had to work harder and harder at controlling his colour. For some reason he felt sad much more often, and it was tough trying to hide all that blue. The same thing happened with the red. He discovered he was feeling angry much more often, and it wasn't easy hiding his anger. He still only felt jealous or envious occasionally, but the depth of his feelings was so great the colour was always very vivid. His delicate, pale shades seemed to have disappeared.

One day the pixie community had a visitor. A very old, very wise pixie from far away came to stay in the King's toadstool for a few days. Everyone wanted to see the wise old pixie, because they'd heard he was a healer. Pixies who were poorly might get better simply being in his presence. And strangest of all, they whispered to each other that the wise pixie had a colour.

Praxis was astonished and very curious. He'd thought he was the only pixie in the whole world to have colours. Now, there was someone else! But try as he might, he couldn't discover the wise pixie's colour. Nobody seemed to know. It was probably, thought Praxis, because the wise pixie changed colours just like he did.

Praxis resolved to see for himself. Although he wasn't ill, and therefore had no right to visit the wise old pixie, he decided to creep in at the backdoor of the toadstool and hide in the shadows. Praxis was very disappointed, for when the wise old pixie came in view, Praxis saw he had no colour at all, he was pure white. First Praxis felt disappointed and sad. Then he began to feel angry, for he felt he'd been misled. Then, as he saw the white pixie glistening and radiant, he began to feel envious, for he himself had never been white.

Praxis worked hard at hiding his colours, but he was so confused and bewildered that all the colours began to peep through, however hard he tried to conceal them. Just at that moment, the wise old pixie turned toward the shadows where Praxis was hiding.

"Why," he said, "what have we here? A rainbow? Come out, little pixie."

Praxis crawled out and looked down at himself. To his horror, he discovered he wasn't just one colour, but was every colour of the rainbow. There were little circles of green, and a great splodge of yellow, large rectangles of blue with dark grey stripes, and a background of red.

"What's happened?" he cried tearfully. "Who am I? Why do I look like this?"

The old pixie smiled at him very gently, and Praxis saw love in the old pixie's eyes. "Once, I was just like you," began the old pixie. "Everybody knew what I was feeling because of my colours, and just like you, I tried to hide my true feelings. But I grew increasingly unhappy and more angry, so I stopped doing that. I decided instead, to work at becoming truly myself."

"Didn't that hurt?" asked Praxis.

The old pixie nodded. "Of course it did, sometimes. Becoming really yourself is a painful process. But having colours is a gift from God. Pixies who have colours are much nearer to becoming their true selves than pixies without colours."

Praxis frowned, trying to understand. "You mean — I'm kind of special?"

"Very special! And do you know, when I'm really myself, my colours all blend to become this brilliant white light you see today."

"Do you mean, you're not always white? Sometimes you're red or blue or yellow?"

The old pixie laughed. "I certainly am! But I've learned to accept myself, even when I'm coloured. And when I'm white, people who come to speak with me are healed, because I'm really myself with nothing to hide my true feelings. One day, you'll be a great healer too, Praxis."

Praxis knew he was right. Suddenly he knew he must spend the rest of his life trying not to be less himself, but more himself. Praxis went away from the wise old pixie, so happy he was bright, shocking pink for three whole days.

Cyril's Taste of Freedom

Luke 9:51-62

> *Jesus suffered rejection throughout his ministry, especially when he started his journey to Jerusalem (this week's reading). He warned would-be followers of the difficult life ahead, for only those with unshakeable commitment would be able to stand the pace. This is a story about Cyril the worm, who longs for freedom. Despite warnings about the tough world outside his comfortable jam jar, Cyril is determined to be free, but he discovers not only dangers but rejection and finds it hard to take.*

Cyril wormed his way through the soil to his brother Toby's side. "Toby," he pleaded, "tell me again what it's like out there."

Toby settled himself more comfortably against the inside glass of the jam jar and began to regale his young brother with his tales of the adventure and excitement of the days before they were caught. Cyril listened with rapt attention. Earthworms have short memories, so young Cyril couldn't remember any other life before the jam jar. But he longed to be free, to be inching through real soil that went on forever and didn't always end at a glass wall.

Toby glanced at Cyril and sighed. "It's not all fun," he warned. "There are all sorts of dangers in gardens. We *could* try an escape plan, but it's safe and warm and comfortable here in our jar and there's plenty to eat. You need to consider very carefully before you make up your mind to enter the big world."

But Cyril wasn't listening. "How, Toby, how?" he cried, bunching up his body and then stretching right out, which was the nearest thing to a jump he could manage.

"All right," said Toby wearily, "just eat. Eat as much as you can so you get really fat. With any luck young Suzie will decide we're too big for the jam jar and will set us free. She might set us down gently in the garden. But," he warned, "it might not be as much fun as you think."

Cyril had made up his mind in the first sentence and hadn't heard. He was already stuffing himself as fast as he could.

It was Suzie's mother who picked up the jam jar a day or two later. "Ugh!" she exclaimed, "these worms are quite disgusting! Fat and horrible! Suzie, I'm throwing them out. You're too big to keep worms anymore."

With that, she tossed the jam jar onto the rubbish heap in the garden. Fortunately, it fell on its side, so Toby and Cyril crawled out as quickly as they could. They buried themselves deep in the compost in case Suzie or her mum changed their minds.

It was a wonderful new experience for Cyril. The warmth and smell of the compost, the tiny insects darting to and fro, and the huge area of this new world all thrilled him. He lost his brother very quickly, but it didn't matter. Cyril felt as if he was in paradise. He kept burrowing and inching and worming his way through the compost, eating soil all the time, and feeling rather proud of all the good he was doing to the soil as it passed through his body.

After a few days, Cyril began to feel lonely. He'd never been on his own before, and he began to long for some worm company. As luck would have it, he discovered a wormery right there in the compost heap. There were dozens of worms of all different sizes and ages. Cyril dived in but came up against a very large worm blocking his way.

"Clear off!" snarled the very large worm.

"Why?" asked Cyril. "I want to come and live with you all. I'm all alone, you see. This is my first visit to your home."

"And your last," sneered the very large worm. "Go away. We don't want you here. You're not part of our family. You don't belong. Get lost."

Poor Cyril was very upset. He couldn't understand why the other worms didn't like him when they didn't even know him. He hadn't done anything to deserve their nastiness. Then he felt angry. He'd like to have stamped all over their silly wormery and crush it — only he didn't have any feet. So he slithered off toward the open garden.

This was better. Cyril set to work passing soil through his body, for that's the job of earthworms. He worked steadily and well, when suddenly four huge prongs of a garden fork nearly pierced him. Before he could collect himself, he was tossed up on a clod of earth.

"Oh!" said an unknown voice. "A lovely fat, juicy earthworm! Just right for the blackbird who lives in the tree." And the unknown voice began to whistle a kind of bird song, calling the tame blackbird. Cyril was terrified. Why did everyone hate him so much? All he was doing was his work, yet now someone wanted to feed him — alive — to a blackbird!

He burrowed into the soil and out of sight as quickly as he could. He began to long for his safe jam jar home again. It might have been boring but at least it was safe. Only Toby had lived there with him but at least Toby didn't hate him, and it hadn't been lonely.

Cyril was feeling very sorry for himself when he heard a terrible noise. A huge shovel came slicing through the soil, lifting and turning it. The next thing Cyril felt was an agonising pain, as the shovel sliced him in half. Cyril lay winded, in two pieces, feeling horribly sick. This must be the end. His enemies had killed him.

Then he wiggled a bit, and to his astonishment, discovered he could move. He was only half his former length, but he was alive and moving. And to his surprise, he spotted his other half also wiggling and moving. He slid over to his other half.

"Hello?" he said tentatively.

"Hello yourself," came the reply. "Hey, it's good to meet you. Do you know, I feel like we belong together. I feel like I've known you all my life."

Cyril grinned an earthworm grin. Suddenly, his life had changed. He was no longer alone and not everybody hated him. How good it was to live in freedom in the garden, with all its adventures and even its dangers. Cyril knew now he'd never go back to the jam jar, for life and work in the garden was very good.

Stepping Out into Space

Luke 10:1-11, 16-20

> *This story follows the gospel story fairly closely, but places it in the setting of space. Ora and Damien discover that a mission to live with aliens leaving behind all weapons and means of communication is very scary. Without those parameters, they would never have learned to be themselves and rely only on the Great Being.*

Damien and Ora grinned at each other in excitement. The time had come — at last! They'd been with the Leader for months and months, waiting for this moment. Not that it had felt much like training. They'd simply lived with the Leader, listening to his stories, hearing about the Kingdom, learning to get along really well with all the other people at Mission Headquarters. Now all seventy of them were ready, the spaceship had docked, and the Mission was about to begin. Ora was glad she'd been paired up with Damien again. They'd worked together before, and there was a calm strength about him that gave her courage. And she was pretty sure he relied on her cheerful good humour too, so it was a good pairing.

She picked up her phaser and checked that Damien had the stun gun. Then she flicked the tiny communicator attached to her collar. "Testing, testing," she murmured into it. She caught the Leader's eye across the crowded landing bay and wondered at the tiny frown that appeared on his forehead. Then the Leader began to speak and at once the whole place fell silent. There was always something compelling about the Leader's words.

"This is it!" said the Leader. "I'm sending you out in your pairs to alien beings you've never met. They don't know you're coming, they don't even know whether or not you're friendly beings. So you must leave all weapons behind. You must not carry phasers or stun guns, and you must leave behind your communicators."

A murmur of surprise ran round the landing bay. "But how shall we manage?" asked Ora. "Suppose the aliens are hostile? How shall we defend ourselves without even phasers?"

Damien added, "And how shall we reach you, Leader? Without any weapons and without any means of communication, we'll be like — like —"

"Sheep waiting to be slaughtered?" finished the Leader. "That's the whole point, Damien. This is your toughest mission yet. You've learned to face dangers and difficulties using all your back-up equipment, now you have to learn to rely on yourselves. So I'm sending you out just like sheep. The risk is that you might find wolves out there! This isn't just about missions to aliens, you know. It's also about you. When you return, you should find you've discovered strength in yourself you never knew existed. Although you won't be able to reach me directly, you'll find you can communicate with the Great Being."

Ora felt very anxious. She hadn't realised it would be like this. She wasn't even sure of the Message. Suddenly she wished the training had been more formal. If only she could have taken notes. Or if only the Leader had given them a blueprint for their wrist computers.

Almost as if he could read her mind, the Leader smiled gently at Ora. "No computers, either," he said. "Just yourselves. You have all the resources you need inside yourselves. When you need to, you'll find them. Now remember, the Message is this: *The Kingdom of the Great Being is close at hand.*

"When you reach a dwelling place, hold your hands out in front of you palms up, and say to the inhabitants: 'Peace be upon this dwelling place.' If a peaceful being lives there, he'll receive the peace of the Great Being and you can stay there. But if not, the peace of the Great Being will be poured into you, and you simply move on to the next dwelling place. When you find somewhere to stay, live as members of that alien family, eating and drinking whatever they eat and drink. You're to live alongside them, exactly as they live, however strange that may feel."

"But Leader," objected Ora, "it won't take us five minutes to say: '*The Kingdom of the Great Being is close at hand.*' What do we do then?"

The Leader laughed, a deep laugh full of fun and humour. Everyone found themselves smiling when the Leader laughed, although they were never sure why. "Well, Ora," he said, "I'm sure you of all people will find something to say! Be yourself. Live the Kingdom. Tell them about me and about the Great Being. Tell them stories, teach them how to worship the Great Being. Heal them."

"*Heal* them?" Ora could hardly believe her ears. "But it's you who is the Healer, not us."

The Leader laughed again. "No, I'm no healer in my own right! It's the Great Being who heals through me. And he'll heal through you too. You only have to ask him. Go on now, all of you. We meet again here in one month. Come back then and tell your stories. Go — and enjoy!"

Damien and Ora were silent as they set off, each occupied by their own thoughts. All their missions had been scary, but this was the scariest of the lot. If they weren't killed, they'd probably starve to death. Ora wondered whether it was possible to live for a whole month without food.

When they reached the first dwelling place, both Damien and Ora found themselves shaking. They each sent a quick, silent thought to the Great Being, "Help!" Then they passed their hands over the usual photoelectric cell, and the door silently slid back, admitting them into a large atrium.

They waited, their hearts thumping. It felt like many eyes were watching them, although they couldn't see anything or anybody. After a while, a huge spider-like creature emerged from the walls and silently glided toward them. Ora stifled a scream. This was like her worst nightmare. She couldn't bear spiders.

Instinctively, her hand flew toward her phaser, but of course, it wasn't there. Ora began to panic. She couldn't think what to do. Then out of the corner of her eye she noticed Damien, his hands held forward, palms up, and she did the same. And the words came: "Peace be upon this dwelling place." The creature didn't move. With a sinking feeling, Ora wondered whether they would be able to communicate at all. Perhaps the creature couldn't understand. But suddenly a wall slid open, and they found themselves propelled into another, smaller atrium, where there were dozens of the creatures.

Despite her fear, Ora heard herself giving the message: "*The Kingdom of the Great Being is close at hand.*" And at once, the creatures began to approach them. Ora kept her thoughts firmly on the Great Being, and to her surprise, found words tumbling out of her mouth. As she began to tell the Leader's stories, she felt an unexpected warmth toward the creatures. When the creatures offered strange looking food and drink, both she and Damien accepted.

It all happened just as the Leader had said it would happen. As they gradually relaxed, Damien and Ora felt the Great Being speaking and acting through them. They stayed for the whole month, and through many adventures, grew to love the strange, spider-like creatures.

When Damien and Ora returned to the Leader, they couldn't wait to relate all their adventures. That night, the whole spaceship was filled with unexpected joy and radiance, for all the evangelists had tales to tell of how the Great Being had supported and helped them just when they needed it.

"I see now," said Ora, "why you made us leave behind all our equipment. I'd never have known the Great Being in quite the same way if I'd been relying on my phaser and computer and communicator. And if we'd had all that equipment, the spider-creatures might have thought we were hostile, no matter we said. We had to rely on the Great Being. There was no one else to approach for help. The Great Being was brilliant and supported us all the way."

"And what's more," added Damien, "the spider-creatures are now worshipping him as well. I don't think it was so much the stories we told them, more us living amongst them and getting along with them despite the huge difference in our species. Anyway, news of the Great Being is spreading all across the galaxy, and because of that, lots of different species are learning to love each other. Interplanetary wars will soon be just a bad memory."

The Leader nodded. "Well done, team," he said. "You've experienced something of the Kingdom on your travels. You've played your part in bringing the Kingdom to the whole galaxy. Now you're strong, and ready to go forward, for you've passed the hardest test of all."

Whose Job Is It Anyway?

Luke 10:25-37

> *The story of the Good Samaritan is an excellent story for children, who immediately understand the moral point. It has already been adapted and rewritten for children many times, so this is a version of the story to bring home the point to adults! In a Family Service or All-Age Worship, I think I would read the Bible story for the children, perhaps asking some children to act it, and then follow up with this story. "Who's Job Is It Anyway?" is aimed more toward adults.*

Mabel hummed a familiar hymn tune as she made her way to church. She always enjoyed her Sunday morning walk. It was one of the few times she felt safe to walk alone through the inner city, for she knew nobody would be up at 7:45 in the morning. Today was a particularly beautiful morning, with blue sky, warm sunshine, and the song of a few intrepid blackbirds who still inhabited the city.

As she turned the corner by the parade of shops, Mabel almost stumbled over a drunk sprawled in a shop doorway. He looked awful, and the stench was vile. Fortunately he was asleep, so Mabel was able to step round him and continue on her way.

But her walk was spoiled. It seemed so unfair that the ugliness of the city should intrude even into the peace of Sunday morning. Mabel couldn't get the drunk out of her mind. She wondered guiltily whether she ought to have done something, although she had no idea what. Fortunately, she knew the vicar and the churchwarden walked the same route, and walked it together. So as long as she was ahead of them, she thought it would be all right. It was their job, not hers.

The vicar and the churchwarden were five minutes late arriving, a good sign. So Mabel relaxed into the familiar atmosphere of church. She gently inhaled the soothing aroma of musty books and recently lit candles. She allowed herself to submerge in the dignified drone of the ancient words and waited with a mild excitement for the comfortable words. Today, "Come unto me all that travail and are heavy laden, and I will refresh you," held a special meaning for Mabel. She drank them in with deep gratitude and felt her anxiety gradually float away from her. God really was in his heaven, and all was right with the world once again.

Mabel walked home on the opposite side of the street, just in case, but couldn't resist a quick peek out of the corner of her eye. To her relief, the drunk had disappeared. The doorway was swept and clean, there was no trace of any problem. Clearly, those in authority in the church had done their job properly. Mabel felt a moment of satisfied pride in the Church of England.

The more she thought about it, the more impressed and proud Mabel felt. Although she was congenitally one of those who scuttled out of the door at the end of the service so as to avoid exchanging more than two words with the vicar, on this occasion something told her she simply must ring and thank him for his efforts. After all, he'd done it on behalf of the whole parish.

Accordingly, she screwed up her courage during the day and rang on Monday evening. The vicar sounded confused. "What man? Drunk, you say? When? I don't remember —" There was a long pause, then, "Oh! Oh dear!"

"What's the matter, Vicar?" asked Mabel. She had never been able to bring herself to call him "John," as so many of the parishioners now did. It sounded far too familiar.

"Mabel," began the vicar, "have you seen today's paper? No? I thought not. It's on page three. Apparently, Sir David Barber — you know? The guy who's done all that work to highlight the dangers single women face in the city — he was viciously mugged on Saturday night. Someone found him at about 8:20 on Sunday morning and called the ambulance. He died in hospital a couple of hours later."

Now Mabel was confused. "What do you mean, 'someone found him at 8:20 on Sunday morning?' You found him, you and Chris Weston, the churchwarden. You must have done. You were late to church."

"No, Mabel. In fact until you rang, I hadn't even made the connection. We were late because — because — well — I got up late. I was out on Saturday night and — oh, well, it doesn't matter. But I was feeling rather tired, and we were rushing, you see. But now you mention it, I do vaguely recollect seeing some chap. I remember thinking he was sleeping it off, drugs or drink or something. We hardly noticed him. Oh dear."

Mabel was outraged. "But it's *your job*! You should have noticed. You ought to have done something. Oh, that poor man. Perhaps he'd be here now if only you'd noticed. If we can't rely on the Vicar, who can we rely on? I really am appalled, Vicar. I must seriously think about changing churches now. I don't think St. Luke's vicar would have passed by on the other side. Have you never read the story of the Good Samaritan? I really don't think I can continue at a church where the vicar doesn't put his Christianity into action. I shall have to start attending St. Luke's. And I'm afraid that means my covenant goes with me." She waited for a moment to give the vicar a chance to dissuade her, but he didn't respond. Perhaps she'd taken the wind from his sails. So she added, "Good-bye," and slammed down the phone, her heart racing.

After a bit, she knocked discreetly next door. Her neighbour looked surprised when she saw Mabel standing there. It was unusual to see Mabel at all. "I wonder if I might borrow your paper," said Mabel. "I believe there's an advertisement that might interest me."

She avidly read the account of the incident. Sir David had been found by some teenage hooligan, probably thought Mabel, a car thief or one of those so-called joy-riders. Well, serve him right. "I don't suppose he stole any cars yesterday," she thought to herself with satisfaction.

She put the paper to one side and rooted out St. Luke's church magazine to check on the time of the early service next Sunday.

Happy Families

Luke 10:38-42

This story is based closely on the various gospel stories of Martha, Mary, and Lazarus but is placed in a modern setting. Martha worries about her young, flamboyant sister but eventually realises she and her sister are so opposite that they have no need for sibling rivalry, for they complement each other.

One of Martha's earliest memories was of her little sister Mary singing and dancing in the middle of an admiring crowd of friends. Mary had always been a dancer, from the time she could walk. Privately, Martha thought she'd always been something of a show-off and ought to go on the stage, for Mary loved an audience.

Martha was very protective toward her brother and sister. She was the oldest of the three, and when their mother had died while Larry was five and Mary was three, ten-year-old Martha had naturally taken over. She'd always loved cooking and homemaking and had slipped easily into their mother's position.

Larry was the quiet one. Being a middle child and the only boy, he was something of a loner. Although he had a group of friends, he rarely revealed anything of his activities to his sisters or their father. He had a great sense of humour, and at times, teased Mary unmercifully. Mary loved him dearly and the whole family adored his company.

Martha sometimes worried about her young sister. When Martha used to cook meals for their father and his friends, Mary would often creep into the room and snuggle up beside her father. She was so pretty, with her long golden hair and dark eyes, that they all accepted her presence. When she began to sing and dance, they'd all applaud. Part of Martha was proud of Mary, but another part felt quite shocked. Martha knew of no other girl who would dare to enter the presence of grown men like that.

As Mary grew older, so she became more provocative. Her dark eyes were enhanced by mascara, her lips glowed with bright lipstick, and her skirts became shorter and shorter to reveal her long slender legs. Now she not only danced for the men but took part in their conversation as well.

Sometimes Martha remonstrated with her. "Really, Mary, you ought to be more careful. You're getting quite a reputation down in the village. Couldn't you keep your hems just a little longer?"

Mary would laugh and cry, "Lighten up, Martha! Come on!" and would grab her older sister round the waist and whirl her around until Martha was breathless and laughing too much to continue scolding.

One day, Larry brought some friends home. He'd come home quite animated once or twice, talking about a group of people he'd met, led by a brilliant healer. "You'll love him," Larry confided to Mary. "He's just your type. When he speaks, we can't help listening. There's something very powerful about him, a kind of restless energy. Yet he has this kind of deep peace inside, which just shines out of him."

Martha bustled about, cooking and cleaning, making sure the house was perfect. When she met the new leader, his eyes twinkled at her and she found herself blushing. He was so nice! But Mary was completely captivated. She hung on every word the leader spoke, she laughed at his jokes, she sat herself at his feet in the position reserved for special students. Martha was embarrassed for her sister but nobody seemed to mind.

The little group of friends clearly enjoyed Martha's cooking and her hospitality, for they came again and again. They fell into a routine of food and discussion, and Mary was treated just like one of the men. Mostly Martha was pleased about that, for she'd never seen Mary so happy or so fulfilled. But it was hard work, looking after them all by herself, and she felt really tired. On one occasion her patience snapped, and she complained to the leader, "Can't you tell my sister to help me? She never does anything. I do all the work around here, and it's just not fair."

The leader had looked at her with compassion and said gently, "You don't really need to go to all this trouble, Martha. I think perhaps Mary's got it right. I shan't be here forever, it's good to listen to what I say while you have the chance."

Although underneath she was pretty sure the leader hadn't meant it that way, Martha had felt snubbed, and had retired to the kitchen hurt.

On another notorious occasion, when they were meeting at a different house, Mary had suddenly appeared in the room with an expensive jar of scented ointment and started to massage it into the leader's *feet*! And worse, she'd then started to cry, and had mopped ineffectually at his feet with her long hair. Martha had been deeply mortified when she heard. Why hadn't the leader stopped Mary from making such an exhibition of herself? Whatever would people think of her sister now?

Shortly after that, all such thoughts fled from her mind, for Larry was taken ill. Martha was worried right from the beginning, but after a couple of weeks when Larry seemed to be getting weaker all the time, she and Mary sent an urgent message to the leader, asking him to come and use his healing powers on Larry.

The leader failed to appear, and Larry died. Martha felt numb. She hadn't felt like this since her mother died, all those years ago. But Mary plunged deep into depression. She'd always been moody, up one minute and down the next, but Martha had never seen her like this. She lay with her face turned to the wall. She refused to wash, refused to talk, and refused to see any of the friends who came to offer their condolences. Most of all, Martha had the feeling her sister was deeply disappointed in the leader. She had admired him so much and been so sure of his love and so certain of his ability to heal. But he hadn't come when he was needed so much. He'd let them all down.

He turned up a day or two later. When she heard he was on his way, Martha slipped on her coat and hurried out to meet him. She was determined to have her say, and she wanted him to know just what effect his absence had had on Mary. She barely waited to greet him but allowed her suppressed anger to simmer. "If you'd been here," she said bitterly, "he wouldn't have died. And you should just see what you've done to Mary."

The leader had looked at her with such love and kindness that she felt tears rising, threatening to overwhelm her. He'd taken her hand and said, "Martha, don't grieve. It's going to be fine, just trust me. Where is Mary? I'd love to see her."

Suddenly, a burden had been lifted from Martha. Suddenly, she knew how the leader valued her, Martha. Suddenly it didn't matter what sort of a person she was, she knew he loved her, just as he loved Mary and Larry. And suddenly she realised how important her role of home-maker was. For she was the strong one, the one who could handle it, the one who could be relied upon and that was special.

She ran home, on air, feeling a joy and a peace she never knew existed. She roused Mary and told her simply that the Master was asking for her. She didn't begrudge the light that immediately shone in Mary's eyes.

For Martha now knew her own worth, and the worth of her brother and sister. She knew the leader would restore Larry to them, but more than that, she knew he would somehow enable each of them to be the best they could be. It didn't matter that each of them was different, for she knew they each complemented the others and that made them a very happy family indeed.

Alice and the Angel

Luke 11:1-13

This is a story about Alice, who asked an angel to teach her how to pray. The result was quite surprising to Alice but gave her an inner resource that would stay with her.

Alice was lying on her back on the grass gazing up at clouds meandering gently overhead when she first saw the angel. She suddenly became aware she wasn't alone. She noticed a slight movement out of the corner of her eye, and when she looked properly, there was the angel, sitting legs crossed on the old tree stump.

"Hello," said Alice. Although he looked a bit like a slender boy or an overgrown pixie, Alice knew it was an angel because he was surrounded by a haze of soft light.

"Hello," said the angel.

Alice thought hard. She'd never met an angel before, so she wasn't sure what to say. But he seemed to be waiting, so Alice said, "Will you teach me how to pray?" She thought that sounded suitably holy.

"Okay," said the angel, "put your hands together and close your eyes —"

"— not that!" interrupted Alice. "I know all about that! I know how to say my prayers. I say them every night. I want to know how to *pray*." And to her surprise, she discovered it was true. She did want to know how to pray.

"Okay," the angel replied, unfazed, "come on, then."

Alice blinked. She was never quite sure what happened next, or how it happened, but she found herself with the angel in a wooded glade. Sunlight was filtering through the trees like lace and playing on the surface of a stream wandering at the foot of a small bank that marked the edge of the glade. Alice just gazed. She thought she had never seen anything so beautiful.

After a bit the angel said, "Go ahead, then. Ask for anything you want."

"What?" said Alice, startled.

"Ask for what you want," repeated the angel.

Alice thought. Then she started a list. It grew longer and longer. She started with a video for herself, and some designer gear, and a CD of her favourite group, and as she named each item, so it appeared in front of her. It was just like one of those game shows. Alice was thrilled. She went on and on, wildly shouting out anything that came to mind, until the glen was overflowing with new possessions. When she couldn't think of anything else to ask for, Alice stopped.

She glanced at the angel. He was looking at her solemnly, but Alice was sure there was a twinkle in his eye. Then she looked back at the huge pile of things in front of her and felt slightly sick. "Don't you want them?" asked the angel.

Alice shook her head. "Can I change my mind?"

The angel shrugged and everything disappeared. Alice sighed with relief. She felt much more comfortable now that she could see the glade again in its natural beauty. Then a thought occurred to her.

"I'd love my gran to be here," she said wistfully. Gran was in the hospital, and Alice had overheard her parents talking in sombre tones about "death" and "not long now."

The angel smiled and immediately, Gran was in the glen. She was in a wheelchair, but she looked fit and well and very happy. As Alice watched, Gran wheeled herself about the glen, exclaiming with delight over the charm of the little stream and the protective strength of the tall trees. As Gran drank in the beauty, so she seemed to grow stronger and stronger.

Alice was so excited she wanted to jump up and down and cry out to her gran, but strangely, no sound came and the old lady seemed not to realise Alice was there. Perhaps it was better that way. Perhaps Gran needed to be able to absorb the healing of the glade by herself. So Alice sat in the shadows, contentedly watching.

As Alice watched her gran, she found herself thinking of other people. As she thought, so each person appeared alone in the glen. Tammy, Alice's best friend, whose parents were splitting up, looked happy for the first time in months. Davy Jenkins, whom Alice disliked and feared and who was on probation for joy-riding, had an expression of wonder on his face. Alice warmed to him for the first time.

This was good. Alice was absorbed in her task and decided to widen her boundaries. She thought of children who were starving or ill-treated in countries abroad and watched them playing delightedly in the glen. She thought of the people she'd seen on television, whose homes had been destroyed by a bomb, and people whose homes had been flooded when the river burst its banks. They all came to the glade.

It took Alice a long time to remember everybody, but it was so exciting to see them all relaxed and content that she didn't mind. At last she said to the angel, "Will it last? Will they stay happy?"

"That's not for you to know," said the angel. "You wanted to learn how to pray. Real prayer doesn't depend on knowing the results. It's about being in God's presence and holding other people in his presence with you. That's what you've been doing this morning."

"I didn't see God," said Alice, surprised.

The angel laughed. "Don't you read your Bible, Alice? No one sees God. That doesn't mean he's not here. You know you're in his presence, don't you?"

Alice nodded. She had never before realised how good it felt to be with God. But she had another question. "I know people were happy here in God's presence, but suppose I want something special for them? Like my gran. I really want God to heal her."

"Then hold her in the waterfall," said the angel. As he spoke, a waterfall appeared, spilling into the tiny stream.

"Won't she get wet? I mean, I don't want her to drown or anything."

"Try it yourself, then," suggested the angel.

Alice ran over to the waterfall and stood beneath it so that the water poured over her, saturating every part of her. Only she discovered it wasn't water. It looked like water, but she didn't get soaking wet — more soaked in the most extraordinary feeling of love she'd ever experienced. She didn't want to come out but more than anything else she wanted her gran to rest beneath the waterfall.

"It's the fountain of God's love," explained the angel, "full of healing because it's living water and it drenches every part of you."

Alice had just one last question. "This has been brilliant," she told the angel, "but how will I ever find this place again? I don't even know how I got here."

"You'll never forget this glade," said the angel. "Any time you want to come here, just find a quiet spot, close your eyes, and picture the glade in your mind. If you ever get fed up with this spot, choose another one. God is present everywhere, so you can choose anywhere you like."

Alice was content. She made to thank the angel, but he had gone. It didn't matter, for Alice thanked him in her mind. She knew he was right, and she'd be able to visit the glen whenever she wanted. She knew the angel would receive her message.

The Marble King

Luke 12:13-21

This is a story about Charlie, who discovers he's very good at marbles and "earns" hundreds of marbles. In the end, he finds friendship and people are more important than possessions.

Charlie Baker was thrilled. He'd just been given a bag of marbles from his grandmother. It wasn't his birthday or anything, but his gran always brought some little gift whenever she came to visit. Mostly it was a few sweets, a little book, and once it was a yo-yo, but this bag of marbles was the best present yet.

There just happened to be a marble craze in the playground at school at the moment, and Charlie had been saving his pocket money to buy some marbles of his own.

He spent all weekend playing with his marbles, rolling them along the carpet, out in the yard, round objects, through tunnels, under obstacles. He discovered he had what his father called "an eye," which meant he was accurate and could hit another marble from several feet away.

On Monday morning Charlie began to challenge other marble owners in the playground. He began to win. Each time he won, he collected a marble from the loser. By midmorning playtime, his little bag was full to overflowing. By lunchtime, his right trouser pocket was bulging with marbles. By the time he went home, his left trouser pocket was bulging too.

Charlie spent the evening sorting his marbles. He sorted them into sizes and colours. He put his favourite marbles in a box in his bedroom, and just kept what he called "the duds" to use the next day.

At school in the morning he set the duds to work. Even using duds, he found he could win every match. He also found he couldn't think of anything else. Throughout the day he dreamed of marbles and again he went home with his pockets and his little bag bulging.

By the end of the week, Charlie had so many marbles he couldn't count them all. His room had several large boxes stacked on top of each other, full of marbles. In the evenings, Charlie would lift out handfuls of marbles and let them run through his fingers, just for the feel of them. But best of all, at school he became famous as The Marble King. Younger children would gaze at him in awe, and whisper to each other, "That's Charlie Baker, the Marble King!" and Charlie would bestow a generous smile on them or nod in their direction.

Just one little problem arose. By now, Charlie had won nearly all the marbles owned by other children, so there was hardly anyone left to play with him. "Give us a few of yours," begged David, his best friend, "then I'll give you a game. I haven't any left." But Charlie shook his head. He'd won the marbles fairly, and he wasn't about to give them away. They were his by right. He'd *worked* for them. David shrugged and drifted off.

Charlie approached different groups of children, but it was always the same story, "Sorry, Charlie, we've no marbles left." As suddenly as it had come, the marble craze was over. Charlie noticed all the other children were already intent on collecting and swapping the little plastic figures from cereal packets.

Reluctantly, Charlie decided he'd better put his marbles away and begin collecting. Next morning he took a plastic Spice Girl into school. "Who wants to swap with me?" he shouted.

But to his horror, all the children turned away. "Go away, Charlie Baker," they cried, "we don't want you around."

Charlie was left all by himself. Nobody wanted to know him, nobody would play with him. When they had a test that afternoon in class, Charlie discovered he knew nothing. He'd been so rapt in his marbles, he hadn't learned a thing all fortnight. Charlie came bottom of the class, and his self-esteem sank very low indeed.

Charlie was miserable. He had boxes and boxes of beautiful marbles, he was still the Marble King, but marbles were useless without friends. He realised that people, especially friends, are more important than things, even marbles.

The next day, Charlie persuaded his mother to drive him to school. He took with him every box of marbles, not keeping any back. At school, he opened the boxes in the playground and poured out all the marbles. "Take them," he cried. "They're free."

With that, he felt free himself, for the first time for several weeks. Happily, before long, his friendships were re-established and Charlie was content once more.

The Big Race

Luke 12:32-40

> *This is a story about Andy, who finds training for a big race quite hard. But one day he meets with a surprise and later is very glad he was ready for it.*

"You coming?" Andy was putting on his trainers and was nearly ready to go.

James yawned. "What for? The race is five weeks away! I don't need to train all that time. I'll start in a week or two."

Andy shrugged and went out to start his pre-breakfast training run. He aimed to run two miles today, then increase half a mile a day. He reckoned he'd be up to ten miles easy by the time of the big race, especially if he put in some hours at the gym as well. It was all right for James. He was the best runner in the school and strong with it. He played Rugby all winter and was always fit. James would probably win the big race anyway, thought Andy, and all this training would be a waste of time. Still, he'd worked out a training schedule and promised himself he'd stick to it, so he might as well begin.

Andy found the first run quite a struggle. He wasn't much of a sports type. It was just that he fancied taking part in the big race with all those people. It looked exciting, and although he knew he hadn't a chance of winning, he looked forward to at least completing the race. Besides, everyone who finished got a medal, and he'd never won a medal for any sporting event.

The training was hard going. James had seemed quite keen on the idea of training together until the alarm clock had woken him that first morning and he'd realised how early it was. Then he'd turned over and went back to sleep, and Andy knew in his heart if he wanted to train, he'd have to train alone. But he'd found it increasingly difficult to get up so early, leaving James in bed. And it became very lonely, running by himself.

The worst time was when he was up to seven miles. His legs and back ached all day after that run, and he'd hardly been able to complete it, he was puffing and panting so much. He wondered then whether to give up. If he could hardly manage seven miles, how would he make ten? And just for some stupid medal! Was it worth all the hassle? There was no one to help or to encourage him. Then he remembered his family and how proud they'd been when he told them about the race, and how they'd all sponsored him for the local hospital, and he gritted his teeth and went on running.

Mostly when he was running, Andy didn't meet anybody else. But when he was up to nine miles, he came across a man lying in a ditch. He wondered whether or not to stop. He didn't like to interrupt his rhythm, and the man was probably drunk. Then he thought ought to stop, for if the man had been lying there all night, he might need a doctor.

He ran over. The man was unconscious, but there was no smell of alcohol, and his leg was bent at a funny angle. Andy made sure the man was still breathing, then he ran a mile further to the nearest house and raised the alarm. The ambulance came within minutes, but it made Andy late for school.

The day of the big race dawned fine and clear. James and Andy started their run together, but James soon pulled ahead. Andy kept on running at his steady pace and enjoyed being part of such a large crowd of runners. There was plenty of good-natured fun and humour, and he soon found himself running with a small group who all ran at about the same pace.

He finished the race in good time and felt proud and pleased to receive his medal. To his surprise, he managed a slightly better time than James, who had run out of steam about halfway round.

His biggest surprise came at the end of the award ceremony. He was called onto the platform by the race organiser and handed an envelope for the hospital. In it was a cheque for 1,000 pounds. Then the organiser announced to the assembled crowd that but for Andy, the race might have been cancelled altogether. He went on to explain that Mr. Glover, the sponsor of the race and owner of Glover and Glover Sports Conglomerate, was a diabetic and when out for an early morning stroll, had fallen into a diabetic coma and rolled into a ditch. If Andy hadn't come along at the right time and stopped to help him, he wouldn't be alive today.

Mr. Glover was wheeled onto the platform in a wheelchair, his leg stuck out in front of him. He shook Andy's hand and thanked him in front of all those people, then told Andy that if he wanted it, there was a good job waiting for him in the firm after he left school.

James was a bit cross when it was all over. He couldn't believe Andy had beaten him. "Anyway," he said, "it was just luck, being there at the right time for that Mr. Glover. And just luck that you finished ahead of me too."

Andy laughed and shook his head. "Not luck," he said, "you have to be ready for surprises in this life. You never know when something's coming your way, so you've got to be trained and ready to deal with it. And you know something?" he added. "Although I found the training really hard and wanted to give up lots of times, I'm so glad I kept going. It was all well worth it in the end."

James snorted and turned away.

Tracey's Temper

Luke 12:49-56

> *The Bible reading says something about the emotions expressed by Jesus when under stress. In this story, Tracey is put under stress by her friends, whose demands clash with her conscience and with the ideals of her family. Her stress erupts into anger, but to her surprise, relationships aren't damaged beyond repair. There are people who can take the anger and still remain friends.*

Tracey was afraid. They were all playing Truth or Dare, and Tracey didn't know which was worst. The dares were becoming more and more scary, and Tracey didn't want to be part of them. On the other hand, she was terrified of being required to reveal her innermost secrets, for she knew perfectly well all the others would laugh themselves silly.

"Your go, Tracey," announced James. "Truth or dare?"

Tracey hesitated. "Oh come *on*, Tracey!" cried the others. "What, you scared or something?"

Tracey shook her head. She was even more terrified of being thought afraid than she was of the outcome. "Dare," she said firmly.

"I know," said James, his eyes gleaming. "I dare you to go into the supermarket and get one of those big bars of chocolate."

Tracey frowned. "I haven't any money, you know I haven't."

James shouted with laughter and all the others joined him. "You don't *buy* it, you wimp," James explained impatiently. "Unless you don't dare," he added.

Tracey swallowed. She knew it was wrong. She didn't want to steal, she didn't even want to play the game, but these were the only friends she had and at times they'd all been nice to her. If she refused, they'd just leave her alone, and she'd find herself with no friends at all. Perhaps it wouldn't matter just this once. What if she got caught? She thought of being arrested, and how her family would feel. She pictured her mother's tears and her father's fury, and she felt miserable.

On the other hand, everyone did it, and none of them had been caught yet. Tracey had shared some of the spoils herself, racing off to the playing field with the others as soon as the goods had been nicked, and sitting giggling in a corner surreptitiously nibbling stolen chocolate and biscuits. It had been good fun and felt really exciting, like an adventure. Although even then Tracey had felt deep inside herself that what they were doing was wrong.

But now it was her turn. She felt under a lot of pressure from the others, who were all eyeing her expectantly. But she also felt under a lot of pressure inside herself, from her own conscience. And she felt under even more pressure from her family, almost as though her parents were right there watching her. Suddenly, Tracey snapped. "This is wrong," she shouted angrily. "I'm not going to do it, and I'm never going to join in again."

There was a stunned silence. Then James sneered, "Scaredy-cat, scaredy-cat! You're just a frightened baby, too scared to be one of the gang. Why don't you clear off?"

To her surprise, Tracey faced him. She was still angry. "You're right, James, I am scared. But I still know it's wrong. And if that's the price of being one of the gang, then I'll just have to stay alone. I don't want to, 'cos I like you guys, but I can't steal, even for you. I wouldn't be able to live with myself."

She turned on her heel, and made to walk away, certain she had ruined everything. None of them would ever want to speak to her again, and they'd probably make her life a misery. But to her astonishment, some of the gang moved across to her and stood with her. "We'll go with you, Tracey," they said. "Bye James, see you later," they added.

Deep inside herself, Tracey knew it was going to be all right. Even if she did lose some friends, she'd make new ones. She knew all the friendships that mattered would survive her anger and her outspokenness. She smiled at her new friends, and they went off together.

Jason's Stand

Luke 13:10-17

This story looks at the cost of breaking rules, even if the rules appear to be manifestly stupid. Jesus broke rules that seem to us stupid in retrospect, but at the time the cost to Jesus was significant, building up until it resulted in his death. For Jason the cost was less but significant nonetheless.

It wasn't until the early summer of his first year that Jason Court felt really fed up with his new school. Until then he'd rather enjoyed it, even with all its rules and regulations, but in the unexpected heatwave of early summer, his patience cracked.

The school rules clearly stated that school blazers must be worn at all times unless permission was given to remove them by a member of staff. One day, when all the classroom windows were open but the temperature was nearing 80 degrees, Jason took off his blazer and hung it carefully on the back of his chair.

It was unfortunate that he chose Mr. Hobbs' lesson. "Court!" thundered Mr. Hobbs. "What do you think you're doing? Put that blazer on immediately!"

"But Sir," protested Jason, "it's so hot. I'm afraid I might faint if I keep it on."

The class tittered appreciatively, but Mr. Hobbs was not amused. His face turned very red. He stood over Jason, very close to him, and hissed at him, "Don't you cheek me, boy! Get that blazer on. How dare you break the school rules!"

Jason wasn't sure what made him do it, but he said loudly and clearly, "No."

The class gasped and waited in excited anticipation to see what would happen next.

Mr. Hobbs seethed. "Get out and take your blazer with you. I'll see you after school for an hour's detention. We'll see if that'll cool you down."

Jason got out and lay on the school field in the sun until break, when half the school crowded round him clearly regarding him as something of a hero. He was determined not to wear his blazer again that day. As it happened, it was so hot that the rest of the staff invited all the class to remove their blazers anyway.

Jason suffered his detention and the next morning spoke to his form tutor. "It's not fair," he complained. "It's a stupid rule. Why can't I take my blazer off if I'm too hot?"

Miss Himpson sighed sympathetically. "I know it's hard, Jason," she said, "but rules are rules. They're made for your protection. You can't just go around breaking them whenever you feel like it. If everyone did that, the school would cease to function. We'd have anarchy."

Jason wasn't sure what anarchy was, but he wasn't about to ask. "You mean we all have to keep the rules even if they're totally stupid?"

"Rules can be changed," explained Miss Himpson, "but you must go through the proper channels. You write to the school council and ask them to consider a change in the rules. That way you'll get a fair hearing. As you know, there are two people from every class on the council, as well as some teachers."

"So if the school council says it's stupid too, the rules will be changed?"

Miss Himpson looked a little sheepish. "Well, not exactly. The council will make a recommendation to the Deputy Head, who will decide whether or not to take the issue further. If he does decide to take it further, the school governors will discuss it and make the final decision."

Jason was aghast. "But that could take years! I only want to take off my blazer when I'm too hot."

"Sorry Jason, that's the procedure. You'll see the sense of rules and procedure when you're a little older."

That evening, Jason carefully wrote his request to the school council. He handed it to his class representative and promptly forgot all about it as the weather changed.

After three weeks of cold weather, when Jason was glad to wear his blazer, the sun shone once again. Jason sought out his class representative. The girl told him the council had supported him, and his application had gone to the Deputy Head.

"Who's that?" asked Jason.

"Mr. Hobbs," replied the girl.

"It's a waste of time, then," said Jason, and the girl nodded. "Actually," she confided, "hardly anything gets changed. It all goes to Mr. Hobbs, then it gets stuck. He just sits on it."

Jason spent the rest of that summer taking off his blazer and hanging it neatly on the back of his chair, whenever he felt like it. The staff grew more and more furious with him. He had detentions by the score, but he refused to give up. Eventually a letter was sent to his parents. Jason explained his position to them.

His father nodded. "Well, Jason," he said, "you are breaking the rules, and you must accept the punishment for that. But I think you have a reasonable case, and you might want to take your protest further by approaching the governors. If that doesn't work, ask to see the Head. As a final resort, you could write to the Press. But sometimes, you have to go on breaking unfair rules to get them changed. Only you ought to be aware that you may find yourself standing alone. Although the whole school treats you like a hero at the moment, you may well find nobody will stand with you if it means *they'll* get into trouble too. So you need to be very strong. You may be threatened with expulsion, and even if you win, you'll probably find your reputation has become that of a troublemaker, and it will dog you all your schooldays."

Jason felt very troubled. He was sure he was right, but he didn't want all the hassle his father had described. He wasn't a natural rebel, and it was very hard to stand up under all the pressure to conform. At the moment he was boosted by the adoration he received from the others youngsters, but if that stopped...

Then he suddenly made up his mind. "I'm going ahead, Dad," he said, "because I'm sure I'm right, and it would help everyone if the rules were changed. What if I get slung out of school? Where would I go?"

His father patted him on the shoulder. "Don't worry about that, son. We'll sort something out if it ever becomes necessary. And Jason," he added, "I'm proud of you."

It continued to be an uncomfortable summer for Jason. But he wrote to the governors, and the rules were eventually changed, and Jason was delighted. The other children all cheered Jason, and some of the teachers looked kind of pleased too. There was a continuing cost, for he suffered at the hands of Mr. Hobbs for the rest of his time at the school. But Jason knew it was worth it.

Beatrice the Bee

Luke 14:1, 7-14

Jesus often told stories against those who were arrogantly certain of their own righteousness. This is a story about Beatrice a tiny bee, who is arrogantly certain she will grow up to be the next Queen of the hive, but things don't turn out quite the way she expected.

Beatrice knew she was a princess, for her mother was Queen Bee. Beatrice had hatched out along with all the other tiny eggs, but even as a larva she had a strong feeling of destiny. She longed for the time when she would be Queen Bee, even though she was aware that would mean her mother the queen had died, for there can only be one queen in a beehive.

Meanwhile, Beatrice practised being queen. She put on airs and graces. She strutted as much as her tiny legs would let her. She fluttered her wings to impress the workers. And she buzzed loudly to impress the drones, the male bees.

As the other larvae began to grow up into workers, they moaned at Beatrice. "You're so lazy, Beatrice," they hummed. "We do all the work. You just lie there and preen yourself, while we're so busy making honey."

Beatrice turned her back and flashed her sting at them. She felt it was beneath her to speak to the workers, but she wanted them to be aware of her power. After all, *she* was a princess and one day would be queen, while they were only workers.

Beatrice grew fat on nectar from her favourite plants in the garden, but she still refused to work. While the workers were busy constructing new cells out of beeswax and cleaning up the hive, Beatrice rested alone, by herself. She was a little lonely, but she was too proud to look for friends, and she was much too posh to visit the new part of the hive to see how the work was going. So she spent her time dreaming of being queen and of all the eggs she would produce.

After a week or two, Beatrice began to feel very tired. She couldn't understand it. She knew worker bees only lived for a few weeks, but the queen could live for several years. What was the matter with her?

Then, to her horror, Beatrice saw the drones gathering round another honeybee. It was a bee Beatrice had ignored, for she thought it was a worker. But now when she looked, Beatrice could see this honeybee was larger than all the rest, even larger than fat Beatrice herself.

Beatrice couldn't help herself. She had to know who the honeybee was. So she lowered herself to speak to a passing worker. "Who's that?" she asked.

The worker stared. "Don't you know? That's Bethany, our new queen. The old queen has died. We're working now for Bethany and waiting for her to produce new eggs and larvae."

"But — but —" stammered Beatrice, "surely I'm the new queen? The old queen was my mother, so I must be a princess."

The worker shook with silent bee laughter. "The old queen was mother to all of us — didn't you know that? You're no more a princess than I am! You're infertile, like us. You'll never be able to produce any eggs, so you can't be a queen. You're a worker bee, Beatrice, but you're no good. You've wasted your life, pretending to be better than the rest of us, and you've nothing to show for it. Now, like the rest of us, your life is coming to an end and you don't even know how to make honey!"

Poor Beatrice. She felt so ashamed. She crawled out of the hive and hid in the petals of her favourite flower, and there she waited to die. But just before her life ended, she felt so very sorry for her foolish pride that some of the workers came with her, to keep her company. "We sisters must keep together," they said. And for the first time in her life, Beatrice was happy and glad to be just an ordinary bee with no airs or graces at all.

Basil's Journey

Luke 14:25-33

> *In this passage from Saint Luke's gospel, Jesus warns of the cost of following him, pointing out that a life of devoted discipleship will make great demands. This theme is picked up in the story of Basil the dog, who retains his loyalty and devotion to his master against great odds.*

Basil was lonely and cold and very tired. He was limping, because his front paw hurt, and his long, hairy coat was bedraggled and matted with the rain. He had no idea how long he had been walking and very little idea where he was headed. He just knew he wanted to go home, and especially to see his owner Mr. Frasier, again.

Basil was a mixture dog, with a bit of this and a bit of that in his make-up, and he hadn't been endowed with much brain. The events of the past few weeks were already growing hazy in his mind. But he remembered Mr. Frasier with a deep, doggy devotion, and he longed to be with him again.

Basil could just remember some good times with Mr. Frasier. He could remember running and running for miles in a wide open space, chasing a ball he kept bringing back and dropping at Mr. Frasier's feet. And each time he dropped it, Mr. Frasier would pick up the ball and throw it again. Basil could remember long walks in the woods, sniffing and snuffling at every delicious scent that teased his nose. And he could remember tidbits of tasty food, occasionally handed to him from Mr. Frasier's own plate.

Basil wasn't sure when it had all begun to change. But over the years, Mr. Frasier had started to use a walking stick and limp a little, and the walks had become shorter and shorter until they gradually ceased. The ball had disappeared and sometimes Basil received not tidbits but a kick and an oath from Mr. Frasier. Having no idea why Mr. Frasier had suddenly begun to mete out such treatment, Basil usually slunk away for a while with his tail between his legs. Then he'd quietly worm his way back and nuzzle Mr. Frasier's hand or lay his head on his lap. Sometimes

Basil would rub against Mr. Frasier's legs, just like a cat. Sometimes Mr. Frasier would lay his hand on Basil's head and murmur comforting words. And once, he started to cry. Basil had licked and licked him, until he felt better and stopped crying.

Occasionally Mr. Frasier would forget to feed Basil at all. And once he forgot to let him out, even though Basil whined and pawed at the door for all he was worth. One day, Mr. Frasier had turned the gas on and forgotten to light it, and both he and Basil had fallen fast asleep until Mrs. Plumpton, their neighbour, had rushed into the house and opened all the windows.

Then had come that fateful day. Mr. Frasier had whistled to Basil to jump into the car. Basil was overjoyed. It felt just like old times! Journeys in the car meant very long walks indeed, sometimes for day after day. He thought he'd heard Mr. Frasier call it a "holiday."

Mr. Frasier drove the car for what seemed like hours. Sometimes Basil heard other cars hooting and felt their car swerve violently, but still Mr. Frasier drove on. When he eventually stopped and opened the door, Basil leapt out and bounded into the undergrowth. He sniffed and snuffled for a bit, then trotted back to retrieve his master. But to Basil's horror, the car and Mr. Frasier had disappeared.

Basil searched high and low for Mr. Frasier all that day, but found no trace of him. In the end, he thought he'd better go home, and he began to follow his nose. He plodded on all night, feeling very hungry, and stopped to search for food and to rest, about dawn. This had been Basil's pattern for months now. He'd walked and rested, stolen food and been chased by angry people. He'd been intimidated by other dogs, and once, only just escaped capture and a visit to the dog pound.

Some dogs, street dogs without homes of their own, had been friendly and shown Basil the best rubbish tips to forage for food. When they'd heard his story, they'd sniffed and barked and told him to forget Mr. Frasier. "Anyone who treats a dog that badly, and then just abandons him, isn't worth remembering," they'd said. But some instinct of loyalty made Basil continue on his quest, and today at long last, he was sure he was near home. Something about the roads and especially the trees and lampposts, was very familiar.

Basil limped into the garden of his home and whimpered at the backdoor. Nobody came, so he lay down in the old garden shed and went to sleep. Each day he stood at the backdoor and whimpered, but nobody came. So each day Basil foraged for food wherever he could, and each night he returned to the garden shed to sleep. Now he'd come this far, no matter what happened to him, he wasn't going to leave until he found Mr. Frasier again.

Basil thought his new life might go on forever, but he'd been spotted by Mr. Frasier's next door neighbour. Mrs. Plumpton put out a bowl of water for Basil, and some dog food on an old tin plate. Basil ate and drank hungrily, and woofed his thanks. He ran toward Mrs. Plumpton, but she didn't seem to recognise him. So Basil lay down at her feet and rolled over on his back with his legs in the air, they way he used to when he was a puppy.

Mrs. Plumpton peered closely at him. "Basil?" she said. "Surely — no, it can't be! It's months since he took you away."

Basil inched his way toward her and began to lick her hand. She stooped down and fondled his ears. "Why, Basil! I really think it is you! You must have travelled thousands of miles and had a terrible time! You look and smell dreadful! Come on, Basil, it's time for a bath."

After his bath, Basil felt like a new dog. Mrs. Plumpton brushed and combed him and all the neighbours gathered round and treated him like a hero. It was rather nice, but there was no Mr. Frasier. "I'll take you to him," promised Mrs. Plumpton. "You see, Basil, he's a poor old man now, and his mind went a bit peculiar. That's why he treated you badly. But he's being looked after in an old people's home, and I'm sure he'll be pleased to see you. Although he doesn't recognise any of us any more."

She took Basil to see Mr. Frasier that afternoon. Mr. Frasier was sitting in a wheelchair, staring into space. He didn't seem to notice anyone at all, so Basil pushed his head into Mr. Frasier's hand and began to lick him. After a moment, a light came into Mr. Frasier's eyes, and he began to respond to Basil. Then he looked up and a slow smile spread over his face. "Basil!" he said. He looked at Mrs. Plumpton and said, "Thank you." And tears sprang into Mrs. Plumpton's eyes, for Mr. Frasier hadn't spoken a word for three months.

Basil was so popular with all the old people that the owners of the home decided to keep him. He had a wonderful new life, petted and pampered by everyone there, but his favourite place was always lying at Mr. Frasier's feet. Mr. Frasier was never again quite as he'd once been, but Basil didn't care. He was home now and that was all that mattered.

When Jodie Was Lost

Luke 15:1-10

> *Jesus told a number of stories to illustrate that when we're lost, God always looks for us and rejoices when we're found. There are no recriminations and no punishments, and our freedom is never curtailed.*
>
> *When Jodie got lost at the seaside and put herself in danger after ignoring her parent's instructions, she was rescued by her parents. She expected to be scolded, but instead she received only expressions of love.*

It was Jodie's first holiday at the seaside, and she loved it. The weather was warm and sunny, and Jodie spent every day on the beach with her mum and dad. Mostly her mum and dad wanted to lie on sun loungers on the sand, with a windbreak to protect them from any breeze, but sometimes they built sandcastles with Jodie. And sometimes they played French cricket with her and with lots of other children who miraculously appeared whenever the bat and the ball emerged from Jodie's mum's large shopping bag.

Sometimes Jodie would wander down to the water's edge and paddle in the sea. "Don't go too far, Jodie," her dad would call out. Sometimes he went right into the sea with Jodie, and they'd swim together, although Jodie could only swim with armbands.

Sometimes Jodie and her dad would walk right along to the end of the beach where the cliffs rose from the water and the sand changed into rocks. Then they'd clamber over the rocks, peering into rock pools and discovering crabs and shells and limpets and tiny fish.

One day Jodie wandered down to the water's edge by herself. "Don't go too far, Jodie," warned her mum. "The tide's about to turn."

Jodie waved to show she'd heard, but she didn't take much notice. She drifted along the edge of the sea, enjoying the feel of the wet sand between her toes and looking out for starfish and crabs. Before long she found herself among the rock pools and became absorbed in peering under seaweed and turning up shells to see what was underneath. She forgot about her mum and dad, and she forgot about the tide until she heard a faint voice crying, "Jodie, Jodie. Where are you?"

Jodie looked up and to her horror discovered she was all alone, standing on a large rock in the middle of the sea. She hadn't noticed the tide coming in all around her. She was terrified. She turned toward the beach and screamed and waved her arms and saw two tiny figures begin to swim out toward her. It was her parents. As they drew closer and Jodie knew she'd be rescued safely, Jodie began to wonder what her parents would say. Would they stop her ever coming to the beach again? Would they say she couldn't go off by herself ever again? They were sure to scold her, and the day would be ruined.

Jodie's eyes filled with tears. But as her mum and dad scrambled onto Jodie's rock, their eyes were filled with love. They both hugged Jodie as hard as they could, and her mum said, "It's all right, love. We're here now. Don't cry."

They had quite a job to help Jodie swim back through the sea to dry land, but they managed in the end. Then they went straight to the ice cream seller and bought Jodie the biggest ice cream she'd ever seen. "Because we're so pleased to have you back safe and sound," explained Jodie's dad. "And you know," he added, "I don't want you to go off getting lost, but even if you were to keep getting lost, I'll always come looking for you. Because your mum and I love you more than anything in the whole world. And whatever happens, we'll always be there for you."

Jodie snuggled up against him and felt safe. Then she wandered down to water's edge again and began to paddle in the waves.

Perry's Little Arrangements

Luke 16:1-13

The story of the Dishonest Steward is a difficult one for adults, let alone children! This story of Perry the elf chancellor and his crafty dealings is simply an attempt to put the parable into a different setting more understandable for children.

Perry skipped and sang as he danced his way to the Elf King's palace. As the Elf King's chancellor, Perry had the most important position in the kingdom, after the king himself. Perry had to ensure the smooth running of the whole kingdom and collect the rent from the emerald, ruby, diamond, and sapphire mines once a month.

The king was a good master, just but generous. All the elves in the kingdom loved him, for they knew he would do anything for them. If any elf was too sick to go down the mine, the king himself would make sure the elf's family had lots of good food to eat and good wine to drink.

Perry liked his job, but he was a trifle lazy. Sometimes he would party all night long, dancing in the fairy ring or playing games with the pixies, and then he was often too tired to get up in the morning and do his job. So he worked out a good scam. When he was delivering the king's good food and wine to sick elves, he'd keep back a few choice items of food here and a bottle or two of wine there for himself. Then, when he was too tired to work, he'd eat and drink and sleep until he felt more like working.

He was aware that some of the elves had discovered his little scheme and mostly disapproved of it, but he didn't much care. As long as he collected the rent from the mines, no one important would know about his other activities. So he skipped and sang as he responded to the king's summons.

When he reached the king's palace, Perry's mood changed, for the king's face was dark with anger. "What's all this I've been hearing about you?" thundered the king.

Perry stood silent and stared at the ground. How much had the king found out? Perry didn't dare answer in case he gave too much away.

"You're fired!" shouted the king. "Go and collect the rent books and bring them straight to me."

Perry gulped and ran out of the room. Whatever was he going to do? He'd never been strong enough to work in the mines, and there was no other work available for elves like him. If he didn't work, he wouldn't eat. At least the king hadn't thrown him into jail. That was something. He was still free, and he knew the king was generous and kind. If only he could think up a scheme to throw himself on the king's mercy.

Perry ran back to his office in the trunk of the old oak tree as fast as he could. He called his pixie helper and ordered him to race to all the mines and urgently summon the overseers to the office in the oak tree. He knew they'd come, for they'd never had such a summons before.

When the overseer of the ruby mine arrived, Perry handed him the rent book. "I've persuaded the king to give you a special bonus for all your hard work this year," he told the ruby overseer. "Your rent is halved. Quick, alter the figures in the book here, before the king changes his mind."

The ruby overseer was delighted and proud, thrilled that all his hard work had been recognised by the king. He made the alterations and sped back to the mine to share the good news with all his workers. There'd be such a party tonight.

Perry did the same with all the overseers from the different mines. He told each of them their rents were halved because of their excellent work, and he told them he himself was responsible for the king's generosity. There was such excitement and delight all over the kingdom, for this was the first time the king had ever made such a generous gesture. The whole kingdom was grateful not only to the king but to Perry for arranging such a good deal.

The last overseer had just disappeared when the king came striding into Perry's office, demanding to know why he was such a long time bringing the rent books. Perry's hand shook as he handed over the books. What would happen now? Would the king have him arrested?

There was a long silence as the Elf King perused the rent books. At last he said softly, "So that's what all the excitement's about! I suppose they're already celebrating my generosity?"

As Perry timidly nodded, the Elf King continued, "You're such a rascal, Perry! If I throw you out now, the whole kingdom will be up in arms against me. And I can hardly tell them there's no bonus after all, when they're already celebrating! I ought to put you under lock and key for this or expel you from the kingdom forever, but — well, the fact is, I love you! All right, Perry, you're forgiven. You can continue as chancellor. Go and join the parties!"

The king walked off, chuckling to himself. Perry could hardly believe his good luck. He ought to be in jail, but here he was, free and forgiven — and he was still chancellor. As he went off to join the party in the diamond mine, he resolved he'd finished with his little schemes once and for all. And he'd try to never let the king down again.

John's Prize

Luke 16:19-31

This story is based on the parable Jesus told about the Rich Man and Lazarus the beggar. It's about John, who is disadvantaged in life, and Michael, who is born into wealth and privilege. One day John wins a very special prize, which acknowledges his loving and caring character, and he realises those characteristics are more important than wealth and privilege.

John was hanging around the gates of the big house, hoping he might catch a glimpse of Michael. They were the same age and had played together when they were small, when John's mum had been the cleaner at the big house.

Once they were a bit older, Michael had been sent away to boarding school, and John's mum had stopped working at the big house because she was ill. John spent a lot of his time looking after her, because she was now in a wheelchair and couldn't do much for herself. Sometimes John was fed up with all the work he had to do when his friends were out playing, but mostly he just got on with it, because there was only the two of them, him and his mum.

Now and then John felt really lonely, and today, at the beginning of the school holidays, he fancied just seeing Michael again and perhaps having a chat with his old friend.

John's spirits lifted as he spotted Michael running down the front steps of his house onto the grounds. Perhaps he could go in and play, as he used to all those years ago. He shouted and waved to Michael, who looked up. But Michael turned away as though he didn't recognise his old friend, and John went rather sadly home to start cooking lunch for his mum.

He heard a lot about Michael over the years. Michael was clever and worked hard at his studies, and won prize after prize in his school, and nationwide. John never studied. He generally felt too tired to concentrate on homework, and he couldn't see the point of it anyway, since he knew he'd have to look after his mum for the rest of her life. Not that he minded. He loved his mum, and they had good times together in their little cottage. But just occasionally, he wished he was Michael.

One day a letter came for John. He opened it in amazement, for he never received any post. The letter told him he'd been nominated for a top award, for the most caring young person in Britain. He was to attend a gala evening in a top hotel in London with his mum, along with all the other children who had been nominated for the award. He and his mum would be taken to London in a limousine, to stay in the hotel overnight, before being brought back the next day.

John was so excited he could hardly keep still. His mum bought them both new clothes for the great occasion, and they travelled to London. They had a wonderful time and sat in the front row at the gala evening. When the time came for the award, John saw with delight that it was Michael and his dad who were to present the awards.

When John's name was called as the overall winner because of the way he cared for his mum all his life, he felt he was bursting with pride. He climbed the steps to the platform and shook hands with his old friend and with Michael's dad. Michael himself gave John the prize and told him it was more important than any of the prizes he, Michael had ever won.

As John went home with his mum, he felt deeply happy. He wasn't rich, and he wasn't clever, but somehow he knew what he had with his mum was worth more than money or brains. He was suddenly glad he was John and not Michael.

Alice's Ambition

Luke 17:5-10

> *When Jesus' disciples asked him to increase their faith, he merely af-*
> *firmed their lack of faith! Then through using the way they treated*
> *their own slaves as an example, he taught them that their expecta-*
> *tions were all wrong. This is a story about Alice, who is so eager to*
> *become a ballet dancer that she goes about it in the wrong way and*
> *learns from her mistake.*

Alice loved ballet. She'd been given a ballet video for her birthday, and she spent hours watching it. When she'd been attending ballet classes for three weeks, she announced to the assembled family that she was going to be a ballet dancer when she grew up.

Alice's mother and father exchanged meaningful glances. "Ballet means a lot of hard work," warned her father.

"And it depends an awful lot on how you grow," added her mother. "Ballet dancers have to watch their diet very carefully, in case they put on too much weight. And some people are just too tall or too short to be professional ballet dancers."

Alice's brother just laughed and made a mock pirouette.

A month later, the ballet teacher announced auditions for ballet school.

"You mean, actually going to a school where all they do is ballet?" asked Alice.

Her teacher laughed. "Not quite! Ballet school is exceedingly hard work, because you have to do all your ordinary lessons and homework, and four hours ballet practice every day as well."

"I want to go in for the auditions," declared Alice.

"But Alice dear," said her teacher, "you've only been learning ballet for seven weeks. That's much too soon to audition. The auditions are really for girls and boys who've been learning ballet for at least three years."

Alice folded her arms and set her jaw. She could be very stubborn when it suited her. "I want to go in for the auditions," she repeated.

No amount of persuasion or reasoning from her family or from her ballet teacher could persuade Alice to change her mind. She'd decided what she was going to do with her life, and she refused to budge. Besides, she was sure she'd be accepted, for she'd studied that video until she knew every move by heart, and she spent hours practising in her bedroom. She worked out a dance that showed all the basic ballet steps, and her teacher taught her the standard routine every entrant had to dance.

When the great day of the auditions came, Alice prayed hard and set off. She danced her best and felt excited and exhilarated as she came off the floor. She waited the whole of the day until the evening for the results.

Three people from the hundred entrants were selected for ballet school. Alice wasn't one of them. She didn't even get a special mention. She went home in floods of tears, certain that her life was ruined. She was inconsolable for a week. She refused to watch the video again and refused to be comforted by her family. Even when her brother bought her a packet of sweets just to show he cared, Alice could hardly bring herself to thank him.

She almost refused to go to ballet class the following weekend, but her mother (who could be stubborn herself) dragged her along. Alice glowered and pouted at her teacher, almost as though it was all her fault.

So her teacher took her on one side. "Look Alice," she said, "it takes a lifetime to become a top ballet dancer. Few people make the grade. You might, because you have real potential and I believe you to be dedicated enough to want to succeed. But you tried to run before you could walk. You weren't ready for that audition, so of course you didn't get any praise for your efforts. One day you might be ready, but there's a lot of hard work ahead of you before then. You need to learn to trust me and respect my judgment. You need to learn that if I say you're not ready, I'm saying it for your own good and not to spite you. All I can offer you is three years hard work. Then, if I think you're ready and have a chance, I'll put you in for the audition again. What do you say? Will you risk it?"

Alice looked at her teacher and found herself nodding. She knew she wasn't going to be a great ballet dancer overnight, but one day, who knows? Perhaps one day her name would be in lights and people would flock to see her dance. Her spirits lifted, and she slipped off the stool and ran to the bar and began to practise.

More Trouble for Praxis

Luke 17:11-19

> *Today's reading is about ten lepers whom Jesus healed. He told them to go and show themselves to the priest and only one leper disobeyed him. He turned back to thank Jesus. This is a story about Praxis, who disobeyed the Pixie King for a very good reason.*

Praxis the pixie was in trouble again. In fact, Praxis was rarely out of trouble. It had all started when he'd begun to be himself. You see, Praxis changed colour when he felt strongly about anything, and so for quite a while he'd tried very hard to be good. But it hadn't worked, for instead of being just one colour, blue or yellow or green or pink or purple or red, he'd become a rainbow of blotches and spots, stripes and circles, all different colours. It had been very embarrassing. So now Praxis was just himself and that meant he wasn't always good.

On this particular autumn morning as he hurried to school with the other pixies, Praxis was a delicate shade of blue. He was feeling rather miserable, because the Pixie King had been very cross with all the pixie children. They'd all been late for school every day for a week, and sad to say, it had been mostly Praxis' fault. He simply couldn't resist paddling in the stream, collecting fir cones, or playing with the squirrels. Now the pixies were all hurrying to school along the path, instead of strolling through the woods, and Praxis didn't like it.

As he dragged his feet at the back of the little group, Praxis thought he heard a cry.

"Hey! Wait!" he called to the others. "I heard something."

They all groaned and the biggest pixie said, "Not now, Praxis! We've had enough of your tales. We must get to school on time today."

"But I did hear something," Praxis insisted. "A cry. I think someone may be in trouble."

One or two of the smaller pixies hesitated, but the big one gathered them all up and shooed them along. "Come on," he said, "I'm responsible for getting you to school on time. Forget Praxis and his silly tricks."

And he called to Praxis, "You'll be in real trouble if you're late. Come on with us." As he saw Praxis' colour change to a stubborn orange, he knew it was useless, so he turned and hurried the group on down the path.

Praxis set off into the woods. It had been a very faint cry, but he was sure he had heard something. He called out as he went. "Hey! Who are you? Do you want help? I'm coming."

After a few minutes he heard another tiny cry, followed by a whimper. He ran toward the noise. As he came into a clearing in the woods, he saw a baby squirrel caught by its tail in a crevice at the base of a large old oak tree. He gently and tenderly freed the squirrel — and then noticed all the acorns lying on the ground. He and the baby squirrel gathered up as many acorns as Praxis could carry. As everyone knows, all pixies wear acorn caps in the winter, but the nuts make marvellous pixie conkers. Praxis determined to hang them on silver fairy twine and have great games with his friends.

Then he suddenly remembered the time, and where he ought to be. He shot off through the woods at top speed and arrived at school out of breath. The teacher was cross and refused to listen to his story, but all the other pixies crowded round him at playtime and were delighted with his gifts of acorns.

But as he dawdled home after school, Praxis began to feel rather nervous. He knew the teacher would tell the Pixie King that he'd been late for school yet again, and he felt fearful of what might happen to him. He felt a little sick, and his colour changed to pale yellow.

Sure enough, as soon as he reached the pixie glade he was summoned before the Pixie King. His legs were trembling but he ran there as fast as he could. To his surprise, the king was smiling and looked really pleased to see Praxis.

"What's this I hear about you?" asked the king.

"I can explain," Praxis said hurriedly. "You see —"

"No need, Praxis," interrupted the king. "There's someone here to see you." And out from the shadows stepped a Mother Squirrel.

"That's him," she said, "that's the pixie who saved my baby's life. But for him, my baby might have died. I'm so grateful to you, Praxis."

Praxis turned bright pink with delight. He hadn't expected anyone to know about the baby squirrel. "So, you don't mind about me being late for school?" he asked.

The king laughed. "Of course not! School is very important, but people and animals are more important than keeping the rules. You were the only pixie who realised that. I'm proud of you Praxis."

Praxis went on his way so happy that he stayed bright, shocking pink for three whole days.

Praxis Looks for Justice

Luke 18:1-8

> *In this story by Jesus, the widow dared to approach the judge be-*
> *cause widows (and women) were protected under the law. She had*
> *the courage to stand up for her rights and even a judge who was*
> *unjust and corrupt eventually gave her justice. God is neither un-*
> *just nor corrupt, so certainly hears and responds to human beings*
> *when they call upon him. In this story Praxis the pixie is looking*
> *for justice and goes through unnecessary work to find it.*

Praxis the pixie was ordering the other pixies around. He was good at doing that and was so enjoying himself that his skin was a bright, bustling pink. But he was a bit bossy as well, so his skin was also tinged with a slightly pompous purple. Praxis' skin changed colour according to his moods, so everybody always knew exactly what he was thinking and feeling.

He'd been brown for a number of days, because he'd been deep in thought. The other pixies always gave him a wide berth when he was in a brown study, because they knew from experience that if they interrupted his train of thought at such a time he'd go blistering red with anger, and then he wasn't very nice to know.

Praxis wanted a pixie picnic, and he'd been trying to work out how to get one. The pixies always had one special treat every year, but the special treat for this year had already happened. Anyway, since it had only been a sing-song with all the woodland creatures, followed by acorn wine, which Praxis was too young to drink, he hadn't considered it to be much of a treat. It was so unfair, he thought. Sing-songs and wine were for grown-up pixies and elves and fairies and woodland creatures and weren't much fun for pixie children. But a picnic! That was different. Praxis could only remember one pixie picnic, years ago when he had been very small, but he had enjoyed it so much that he'd always wanted another one. The very thought of the delicious food that all the different woodland creatures would bring made his mouth water, and there were bound to be games and sports and races. Terrific!

But how could he get one? He thought of being so naughty that he was taken before the Chief Pixie — that had happened on a number of occasions before — then he could ask about his picnic. Somehow, if he'd been that bad, he didn't think the Chief Pixie would listen.

He thought of climbing as high up the old oak tree as he could, then dropping down right in front of the Chief Pixie's toadstool, so that when the Chief Pixie heard the crash and came running out to see what had happened, he'd feel so sorry for Praxis that he'd grant any wish. But the trouble with that was that he might get really hurt, then he wouldn't enjoy a picnic even if they had one.

He thought of finding a big leaf and writing a letter on it, asking the Chief Pixie for a picnic. But he couldn't write very well, and it sounded like hard work, so he didn't bother. He thought of being so good and so helpful that the Chief Pixie would reward him for his efforts. But the thought of being good for a long time filled Praxis with horror, and anyway, he thought there was no guarantee that he'd be rewarded at all, so he certainly didn't want to be good for no reason.

Then Praxis had a brainwave. He'd find the smallest, youngest, cutest pixie and send her to the Chief Pixie with a message. Surely even the Chief Pixie wouldn't refuse then? So Praxis was busy now, ordering all the pixie children to line up in front of him so that he could choose the cutest and send her on her way. But to his surprise, he found it really difficult. He discovered that all the little pixies were cute, and he couldn't pick out any one of them who was cuter than any other.

But with that came his second brainwave — they could ALL go, one after the other, so that the Chief Pixie really got the message. And he couldn't possibly be cross, because the chosen pixies were so small.

Praxis strode up and down the line, giving orders to the little pixies. He made them practise over and over again, until each of them knew exactly what to do and how to do it. Then he sent them on their way and hid behind a mushroom to see what happened.

Starting with the biggest and ending with the smallest, all the little pixies formed up in a line, as Praxis had instructed them. Then they marched off to the Chief Pixie's toadstool. The first pixie rapped on the door, and when the Chief Pixie emerged said, "Chief Pixie, you are the wisest and noblest pixie in the whole wood. Please give us little pixies a picnic, for that would be a wonderful gift for us."

The Chief Pixie looked too astonished to frown and promised to think about it. Then he went back inside and closed the door. A moment later, the second pixie rapped on the door and delivered the same message. Again the Chief Pixie promised to think about it. By the time the fifth pixie had rapped on the door with the same message, the Chief Pixie was beginning to look very puzzled and his frown was beginning to come back. By the time he saw the twelfth and last pixie, the tiniest of them all, standing there, his frown was very black indeed. But he couldn't be cross with the tiniest pixie, who had forgotten her lines.

Then the Chief Pixie stood outside his door and roared, "Praxis!" in a voice that sounded so much like thunder that all the little pixies shivered. Even Praxis himself discovered that his knees were knocking. How had the Chief Pixie known he was behind the pleas? With his head bent, Praxis shuffled forward.

"So!" roared the Chief Pixie. "What's the meaning of this, Praxis?"

"It...it wasn't f-fair," stuttered Praxis. "Sing-songs are for grown-ups. I only wanted a picnic." Then he added hurriedly, "For all the pixie children."

The Chief Pixie squatted down until he was the same height as Praxis, which made Praxis feel even more uncomfortable. But to his astonishment, the Chief Pixie was looking at him with kindly eyes, and his voice was really gentle. "Praxis," he began, "you can have your picnic. But you know, you only had to ask. Next time you want something from me, just ask. I might say no or I might say yes, but you need to ask me first. And because you made all these other pixies do your work for you, you're going to have to do something for me."

Praxis sighed and his skin turned a sad blue. What would his punishment be this time?

"I want you to organise all the games for the picninc," said the Chief Pixie. "I'll organise the food, you arrange the games. Will you do it?"

Praxis' eyes suddenly shone. That meant he could have all his favourite games! He nodded his head as fast as he could, and he was so happy that his skin turned bright, shocking pink for three whole days.

I Will If I Want

Luke 18:9-14

It isn't easy to teach children how or when to say "sorry." Some children are told so often that what they do is wrong, they grow up believing they have no worth and spend the rest of their lives with low self-esteem and constantly apologising for their very existence. Other children are never corrected and grow up with no idea of boundaries or even of right and wrong. We need to help children to grow up to be confident in themselves but also to learn true humility, to recognise that sometimes they can be wrong, but that despite mistakes and failings, they are still worth more than the whole world, especially to God. In the parable, the Pharisee has no real idea of boundaries or of right and wrong, and therefore cannot say "sorry." But the tax collector, acknowledged to be a thief and a cheat by virtue of his job, has somehow learned true humility. This story attempts to explore these issues in a very simple way.

Mrs. Bushman sighed. "Don't pick up such large walnuts, Will," she scolded.

"I will if I want," muttered Will, sulkily.

Fortunately his mother didn't hear him. She was busy explaining to him why he should always look for smaller walnuts until he was a fully grown squirrel. "The larger the walnut, the heavier it will be to carry," she said. "And if the walnut is too heavy for you, something dreadful will happen."

Will made a face at her behind her back. He was fed up with always being told what to do and how to do it. Besides, he was the biggest of all the young squirrels, and he knew he was strong enough to carry any walnut he liked. His mother didn't know anything. She always treated him just like the youngest squirrel instead of the oldest. He shook his bushy tail and scampered out of sight of his mother so that he could do exactly what he wanted without any hassle.

Will's best friend Nigel Nutman was busy burying hazelnuts. "Look at my hoard," boasted Nigel. "I've got more hazelnuts than even the grown-up squirrels. I've got nearly as many as my dad, and he's the best Nutman any squirrel has ever known."

Will sniffed. There were times when he didn't much care for Nigel who was rather prone to bragging, but Will envied him too. Nigel seemed to be able to do anything he liked. "You're not supposed to do that," retorted Will. "You know you're only supposed to gather one armful a day, so as to leave enough for everyone else. The teacher said so in school today."

"Pooh!" cried Nigel. "I don't care what anyone says. I do as I like."

"I bet you wouldn't say that if your dad knew what you were doing," said Will, a little in awe of such daring.

"He wouldn't care," swaggered Nigel, "my dad lets me do what I want! My parents never stop me from doing anything. I can do as I please."

Will kicked hard at a hazelnut and ran off. It wasn't fair. Why should Nigel spend all his time doing exactly as he pleased, when he Will, had always to obey his parents and do as he was told? Will resolved to be more like Nigel and to start doing just as he wanted without taking any notice of anyone.

That evening Will's father said sternly, "I don't want you to see too much of that Nigel. He's a bad influence on you."

"I will if I want," muttered Will and felt better. But he said it under his breath so that his father couldn't hear. Then he started to crack open a delicious walnut with his sharp teeth.

"You should bury that walnut for the winter when you'll need it. Don't eat it now," warned his mother.

"I will if I want," repeated Will, and his eyes flashed angrily. Mrs. Bushman looked up sharply at his tone, but she didn't say anything. Her big brown eyes looked kind of sad, but Will didn't pay any attention to that. He made sure his father had gone out and went on eating the walnut. Then he ate more walnuts until he felt ready to burst. His mother looked at all the empty shells on the floor, but she didn't say a word.

It was quite difficult to run after eating all those walnuts, but Will was big and strong so he didn't worry too much. When he spotted the largest walnut he had ever seen, naturally he made straight for it. He picked it up carefully in his front paws and began to carry it back toward his special hiding place, where all his walnuts were buried. But his foot hit a buried hazelnut and he tripped. He staggered a little, and then found that there were hazelnuts buried all over the place. It was Nigel Nutman's secret hoard, and it seemed to stretch everywhere. The ground was so uneven that Will couldn't keep his balance. And he'd eaten so much that he fell heavily. The giant walnut rolled out of his paws and away, but Will found he couldn't get up. His leg was twisted under him, and it hurt.

Will didn't know how long he lay there unable to move. He got more scared as the daylight began to fade and night began to fall. He began to shiver with the cold, and a tear rolled down his cheek. He tried calling out, but there was no one to hear. Not even Nigel Nutman, who was probably burying even more hazelnuts elsewhere.

Then at last Will spotted a light in the distance and began to shout with all his might. The light came nearer and nearer and at last Will's mum and dad came into view. Will thought they'd be cross with him, but they were so kind and gentle and concerned that Will felt over-whelmed with their love for him.

Nigel was unrepentant when he found out what had happened to Will. "It was your own fault," he said airily. "You should look where you're going. It wasn't my fault. I've done nothing wrong."

Will thought very hard about what his mum and dad had said to him earlier in the day. It all suddenly began to make a bit of sense, and he felt very ashamed of the way he had behaved. "I'm sorry, Mum," he whispered. "You were right. The walnut was too heavy for me. I've been really stupid." And he said to his dad, "I'd never noticed before what Nigel was really like. He's not my best friend after all. But poor old Nigel! His mum and dad don't care what he does, so he doesn't know how to behave. He's not a very nice person, is he? And he doesn't even know when he gets things wrong."

Will thought his dad might give him a lecture, but he didn't. His mum and dad hugged him tight.

"We love you, son," they whispered.

"And I love you too," Will replied, "but I've only just realised how much!"

Philip's Ears

Luke 19:1-10

> *Nobody liked Zacchaeus and most probably despised him. Jesus didn't notice any of that. He simply wanted to be Zacchaeus' friend. That changed Zacchaeus' life and he became a new person. In this story, Philip is despised and unpopular because of his big ears. However, his life is changed when somebody is nice to him and genuinely wants to be his friend.*

Philip first realised there was something odd about himself when he was quite young. He remembered the incident well. He was out in the park with his mum, playing on the swings when he overheard two ladies talking. They were right over on the edge of the park, but Philip had been blessed with very acute hearing.

"Just look at that poor little chap," one of the ladies was saying to the other. "What a handicap to go through life like that."

"Oh! Dear me, yes," replied the other. "Poor kid."

Philip didn't really understand what they were talking about, but he was interested in this "poor kid," so he looked round. There were no other children in the park, and he realised that the ladies were looking straight at him. He didn't take much notice at the time, being absorbed in the swing, but later on at bedtime he asked his mother what a "handicap" was.

His mother frowned and asked him where he'd heard that word. When Philip explained, his mother grew very upset and angry and gathered him in her arms and told him not to worry about silly people who didn't know what they were talking about, and that there was nothing at all wrong with him. Then Philip knew he must be odd in some way.

He realised how different soon after he started school. One of the other children asked him when he'd been hung on the clothesline by his ears, and whether it had hurt. At home the child's parents had been discussing Philip hanging by his ears so the child wanted to know from Philip what it felt like. Philip felt angry and pushed the boy, who fell over and hurt his knee. After that the other children gathered round, and they soon started laughing at his ears and pointing to them and jeering at him.

That evening Philip looked at himself carefully in the mirror and realised that his ears were quite large, and that they stuck out from his head at right angles. "Don't you worry," said his mother, comfortingly. "I love you, and anyway, Prince Charles has ears just like yours, so perhaps you're from royalty."

The next time the children started to pick on him, Philip retorted that he was from royalty and that Prince Charles was probably his uncle but that only made the children laugh at him even more. Worse, they started calling him a liar.

After that, Philip kept to himself. He kept away from the other children and became known as a weirdo and a loner through the school as he grew up. He spent a lot of time playing fantasy games on the computer, because it was great and he could do that alone.

When he moved on to high school at the age of twelve, Philip was already quite tall. It stood him in good stead, especially when some of the older boys tried to bully him. Philip growled at them and punched one of them on the nose and made it bleed. They left him alone after that but kept taunting him from a distance. The taunts were always about his ears. Philip tried not to care, but it hurt him deep inside.

By now, Philip was used to being lonely, but he gradually became angry and morose as well, and people started to become afraid of him as his reputation for using his fists grew. Philip was glad. That was just as he wanted it.

Then a new girl started at the school. Amanda was stunning and nice with it, and she soon collected a crowd around her of boys and girls. She quickly became the most popular person in school.

Philip ignored her until one day his sharp ears overheard her discussing the latest fantasy game. Philip was amazed, because as she spoke, it was clear Amanda knew what she was talking about. He slid a little closer and hung about on the edge of the group wanting to hear but not wanting to be part of the crowd.

Suddenly Amanda pushed her way out of the crowd until she was standing beside Philip. "I want to be your friend, Philip Marsh," she announced. Philip gaped at her with his mouth open and waited for the roar of laughter. He was sure she was mocking him, she had to be. But nobody laughed. Rather there seemed to be a kind of breathless hush. "Huh!" snorted Philip rudely, not trusting her at all, and he started to walk away as quickly as he could.

But Amanda kept up with him. They walked until they were clear of the crowd, then Philip flopped on the grass at the edge of the school field. "Why don't you go away and leave me alone?" he muttered.

"Because I like you," replied Amanda.

"Well that's a first," Philip said, cynically. "'Cos nobody else does." He soon found himself responding to Amanda as she talked about fantasy games, and as he listened, he began to warm to Amanda. By the time they had been chatting together for an hour, Philip began to feel he really had met a friend for the first time in his life.

It was the start of a new life for Philip. As his friendship with Amanda grew, so Philip began to come out of his shell. Because he was with Amanda, he seemed to be accepted by the other youngsters as well, and he suddenly realised what a wonderful feeling it was to be part of the crowd. He still wasn't quite sure whether this brilliant new life would last. Somehow or other he kept expecting something to burst the bubble.

One day he said to Amanda, "How come you like me? Nobody has ever liked me before, well, except my parents, and they don't count. When people look at me they see a freak with huge floppy ears like an elephant. How come you don't mind all that?"

Amanda was surprised. "I've never noticed your ears," she exclaimed, and she leant over to have a good look at them. But somehow, Philip didn't mind. Then she continued, "I suppose they are quite big, but that's why you hear so well. I've never met anyone before who can hear like you. Why, if I'm right over the other side of the school field and I whisper, you can pick it up. No one else can do that. Anyway, who cares about ears? That's just silly. You and I like the same things, and I just like hanging out with you, that's all. Anyway," she added, "have you never noticed that I'm a bit weird too?"

"You?" said Philip, "never! You are the most popular person in school."

Amanda laughed. "Only because I don't allow my weirdness to get in the way, so nobody else bothers about it either. I bet you haven't even noticed it, have you?"

Philip shook his head, and Amanda spread her fingers. For the first time, Philip noticed a thin web of skin between each finger. He took her hands and gazed at them wonderingly. "You see?" said Amanda. "All the kids used to call me Froggy or Fishface, but I refused to feel hurt so I just laughed along with them. Then they forgot and nobody really notices now."

Philip brought her hands to his lips and kissed them gently. "I love you," he whispered, "and I don't care about your hands. And do you know, for the first time in my life I don't care about my ears, either. I know now that it's the person that matters and anything else is just — silly!"

They both laughed.

He Who Laughs Last

Luke 20:27-38

Those with silver tongues who were skilled orators tried to use their talents with words to humiliate Jesus and hide from the truth, but the truth lies deeper than words.

Henry Hyena had a problem. He was quite popular with the whole hyena pack, because he could make them all laugh. Henry was full of jokes, and on a dark night you could hear all the hyenas howling with laughter because of Henry's humour. Apart from his jokes, nobody ever listened to anything Henry said.

It was all Clarence's fault. Clarence was the biggest and strongest of the hyena pack, so he had declared himself king and all the hyenas did everything he said. What's more, Clarence was very good at speaking. Not just talking to his friends, but speaking to the whole pack together. There was something about the way he used words that made the whole pack want to follow him.

Everyone except Henry, that is. Henry didn't trust Clarence. He heard all Clarence's fine words, but when he thought about them afterward, he realised they were empty words. They didn't mean a thing. Henry tried to point this out to his friends but nobody would listen. They were all too busy hanging spellbound onto every word Clarence the king uttered.

One day Clarence gathered the pack around him. "Hear this," he began, "all this territory should belong to us hyenas by right. We were here before any of the other animals. This territory belongs to us. They are intruders. They should find their own land, not steal ours. I say, get rid of the outsiders!"

Immediately the pack took up the shout, "Get rid of the outsiders!" There was a terrible baying and barking from the throats of the hyenas, but no laughter. They began to prepare for war against the other animals.

Henry was appalled. "Listen," he tried to say, "we can't just —" but Clarence cut him off.

"If you're afraid to stand up and fight with your brothers and sisters, stay behind," Clarence barked.

"No, I —" Henry tried again, but the pack turned on him and began to bite and scratch him. Henry slunk away, his tail between his legs. He was very worried. He knew the pack would stand no chance against the lions or the buffalo or the wildebeest, no matter what fine words Clarence used. And none of the other hyenas were as strong as Clarence. They wouldn't be able to do what he wanted. Anyway, Henry quite liked to have the other animals around. They sometimes allowed the hyenas to finish the meat on any carcasses they had killed, and Henry was afraid that without the other animals, there would be no meat.

He went round to each of his friends in turn to plead with them not to follow Clarence. But none of them would listen. They were all starry-eyed about Clarence the king and took no notice of Henry, except to laugh at him.

The great day of the fight came. Clarence led the pack out to battle against the other animals. But Henry stayed behind. The pack called him unkind names and said he was a coward and jeered and laughed at him. Henry felt bad. But he knew someone should be around to pick up the pieces after the battle, for he feared that many hyenas would die or be horribly injured.

There were terrible sounds of a huge animal war that day. Henry listened and shivered at the screams and cries. At the end of the day a sorry pack of hyenas returned home. Many had died and nearly all the rest were injured. Henry went round to each one, binding up their wounds, talking to them quietly and kindly and finding them fresh meat to eat. When he'd finished, he told them jokes until they began first to smile a little and then to laugh again.

Clarence the king had been trodden underfoot by a huge elephant and was never heard of again. The next day, each of the pack came up one by one to Henry. "We believed in all his wonderful words," they said, "but you listened to your own inner voice. You tried to tell us the truth, but because Clarence spoke so well, we refused to hear you. Now we're so very sorry. Henry, you make us laugh and you're good inside. We want you to be our king so that we can always live with the other animals as God intended we should."

So that day Henry became hyena king, and they all lived happily ever after.

The Trouble with Trevor Reeves

Luke 21:5-19

> *Jesus' disturbing words, forecasting doom and gloom for the world in the near future, may be a reflection of the doom and gloom hanging over him at this point. His ministry is all but over. He is arrested and executed soon after this. Our behaviour and attitudes are often the result of discomfort in our own lives, although we rarely recognise the connections.*

Trevor was in trouble again. He had never been in trouble in year six, but now he was in year seven everything had changed.

It seemed to start with the new school. Trevor had arrived on the first day proud and smart in his new school uniform, but one of the teachers had shouted at him for having his blazer unbuttoned. Trevor had stared in amazement, his mouth open. He couldn't believe anyone could be so stupid as to care whether or not he wore his blazer undone.

"Do your blazer up boy, don't stand there looking like a half-wit," the teacher had snarled.

Stung by such unkind words and by automatic reaction, Trevor had stuck his tongue out. The whole class had sniggered loudly, and the teacher had erupted. Trevor had been dragged off before the Head, who had told him the school wouldn't accept boys who didn't know how to behave and that it was the first time in his (the Head's) experience that a boy had been marked down as a troublemaker on his very first day. From now on, the whole staff would be told to watch out for Trevor Reeves.

Trevor felt angry and upset. He felt much more angry and upset when he discovered every teacher was picking on him. Never before had he been in a situation where he was disliked and distrusted before anyone knew anything about him. Within a week, he decided he hated school and he was never going to try again.

There were compensations. He soon gained a reputation in the school for being a "hard man" and the other children looked up to him.

He was never bullied, for the bullies were afraid of someone who was in trouble as often as Trevor. Many of the teachers soon ceased to care whether or not he did his homework, so he seldom bothered.

His form teacher was quite nice. She seemed more gentle than the others. One day, after a particularly bad week, she called Trevor over. "Look, Trevor," she began, "if this goes on, the Head will write to your parents. What will they say?"

Trevor laughed, but it was an angry laugh. "They won't care! My dad's left home anyway, and my mum's all wrapped up in her new boyfriend. Nobody cares, and neither do I, so there!"

He expected the usual irate response, but Mrs. Weldon simply paused and looked at him. Eventually she said, "When did your dad go, Trevor?"

Trevor was taken aback by the kindness in her voice, and before he could do anything about it, tears began to pour down his face. He was glad there was no one else to see him. Mrs. Weldon did nothing. She just let him cry and cry until he felt quite drained. Then he said in a muffled voice, "He went away on holiday in the summer, and I haven't seen him since. I don't know where he is."

"Have you asked your mum?" asked Mrs. Weldon.

Trevor nodded. "She won't tell me anything. She just says she's glad he's gone and we're better off without him. Her new boyfriend's all right, but he's not my dad."

"Trevor," said Mrs. Weldon, "did you know that when something awful happens in your life, it colours everything you think or do? Do you think your behaviour in school might have something to do with your dad leaving?"

"Of course not," shouted Trevor. "That's the school's fault! All the teachers pick on me. It's not fair! It's nothing to do with my dad!" But he found his tears were starting again.

Mrs. Weldon arranged with Trevor that he should see the school counsellor once a week. Trevor wasn't very keen to go, but once he started he found he could tell the counsellor anything he liked. Over the weeks he poured out all his grief and anger and frustration about his parents, and he found to his surprise that the teachers gradually stopped picking on him. He began to concentrate again on his schoolwork.

At the end of the year, at Presentation Evening, Trevor was called onto the platform in front of all the parents, all his year, and all the staff. To his astonishment, the Head presented him with a silver cup. "This is my special award," said the Head. "It's given for different things each year. This year I present it to Trevor Reeves for showing great courage in personal difficulty and for being the most improved pupil in the year."

There was enormous applause for Trevor, and he smiled at his mum and her boyfriend, who were sitting in the front row. But he went over to Mrs. Weldon. "You should have this," he said. "You were the only one who realised I was so naughty because I was so unhappy. I didn't even realise it myself. But you understood, and you cared enough to help me straighten things out. You know what? I'm seeing my dad next week!"

Mrs. Weldon smiled. "It's no trouble, Trevor," she said. "In fact, it's been a pleasure to have you in my class. May you go on from strength to strength."

Trevor knew he would.

King Agadir

Luke 23:33-43

> *King Agadir was a good and wise king. Sometimes it seemed he was too wise, for occasionally one of the courtiers or the young princes would challenge him. They seemed to think that being a king was all about riding on a shining white charger and using a sword. They would often show off their fencing skills, especially in front of the prettier princesses.*
>
> *King Agadir would just laugh. He remembered the times when he had been a young and brash prince himself. He too had had no idea of the real qualities needed by a king. His father had sent him on a time journey to find out for himself the qualities required to be a king. He tried to tell the young princes something of his story.*

"I found a king," said Agadir, "riding on a —"

"— a donkey! Yes, we know," finished the young princes, groaning. "we've heard it all before! But that wasn't a real king. That was just a man people wanted to be king. Real kings are born. Only princes can be real kings."

"So which one of you will be king?" asked Agadir looking from one to the other. "You can't both be kings. You may be my sons, but only one of you can be king. Which will it be?"

The boys looked at each other. They were grinning, for they'd heard this conversation before. "Whoever lives the longest!" said the eldest prince cheekily. "May the best swordsman win!"

"Did I ever tell you the end of the story?" asked Agadir. "You see, I thought the same as you, to start with. I laughed at the man on the donkey. But then I went around with him for some years. I discovered he was the kindest, gentlest, most lovely person I had ever met. And he was so brave! I've never met anyone before or since with such courage."

"Not much courage in riding on a donkey!" sniggered the youngest prince, with a sideways glance at his brother.

Agadir looked at his son with some distaste. There were times when he wondered whether he inhabited a different world from his sons. "I saw that same young man in remarkable acts of courage," said Agadir. "There was one occasion when he went into the temple and threw out all the merchants. He overturned all their tables and scattered their wares on the ground. He drove them out with whips. He called them all thieves, because a temple should be a place of prayer. After that, the religious leaders were out to get him. He knew they were out to get him, but he went on teaching and preaching quite openly."

"What happened?" asked his oldest son, interested in the story despite himself.

"He was eventually arrested," said Agadir. "They picked him up at night in a garden. They rigged a trial. Even then he could have saved himself. He had only to protest his innocence, and the governor would have set him free, but he refused to say a word. Whatever they did to him, he simply stayed silent."

"He must have been stupid!" exclaimed the youngest prince.

"The really courageous people in this world," explained Agadir, "are fools for love. They love another person so much that they have a burning desire inside for the person they love. They will do anything for that person. They will even die for them, if necessary. Some parents love their children like that. But that particular man didn't only love his own family, but everybody he met. Rather than sell them down the river, or tell any lies to save his own skin, he chose to die for all those people he loved."

The boys were quiet now, struggling to understand how anyone could be so foolishly brave. Their father added, "That's the mark of a true king. Someone who loves all his people so much that he will go to the stake for them. Now which one of you said you would be king?"

The princes grinned at him sheepishly, for they weren't bad lads at heart. They ran off to practice fencing with their swords, but somehow it didn't seem quite so important now. Each of them wondered in his heart whether he was really brave enough ever to be king.

Lectionary Index (Cycle C)

Scripture Index